KINGS AND BONES

JULIETTE CROSS

Editing by Corinne DeMaagd

Cover Design by Thander Lin

Cover Page for *KINGS AND BONES* and "A Beast Fae's Bargain" by Krysten Kruse

Character Illustration by Panna Mara

Originally published in THE LOVELY DARK anthology.

PROLOGUE

MURGHA

"Don't cry, Mur."

My sister rocked me in her arms on the porch of our inn. Our father was in the yard, yelling obscenities at Mama. Her cheeks streaked with tears, she was on her knees, begging him.

"Please, Phestys. Let me stay." She had her hands clasped together as if in prayer, her pretty, dark hair having come loose from her braid. "The girls need me."

"The girls don't need a whore to teach them nothing."

Towering above her, he threw her satchel at her feet, the one she used to harvest herbs in the forest. But it was bulkier now, filled with the clothes I saw Papa stuff inside minutes ago.

"I know. I'm so sorry. I never meant..." She shook her head, biting her lip, her eyes full of pain and sorrow. Then her gaze flicked to me.

"Meant to what?" Papa leaned down and snarled, "Spread

your legs for a moon fae bastard? I think you meant that well enough. Proof is right there." He pointed to us on the porch steps. No, not to us. Just me.

Mama shook her head. "You don't understand."

"Nor do I care to. You was gone three days this time, woman. Out whoring again, I suppose."

She shook her head but didn't deny it aloud.

"You're no good to the girls or me. Get you gone." He waved his hand, shooing her from the yard.

When she continued to shake her head and beg, her sad eyes flicking to me and Tessa, he picked her up by the arms.

"I said"—he tossed her out the gate where she fell in the dirt lane—"get you gone!"

I dug my fingers into Tessa's waist where I held her close, but she didn't complain. She kept petting my hair, trying to soothe me.

Papa stood with arms crossed at the foot of the stepping stones that led to our inn, scowling down at Mama. She hauled herself off the ground and heaved the satchel over her shoulder. Then she looked at me and Tessa.

Though her hair was mussed and her face pink and streaked with tears, she looked like she always did when she brought us into the forest to collect sorrel, milk thistle, juniper, or figwort. She'd taught us all of the plants with special properties to heal and to make our food taste good. She did so many things to make life more lovely, to make us feel loved. And now Papa was sending her away.

She offered us a sad smile and watery words of, "Be good, my sweet girls. I love you."

Then she turned and walked down the path leading out of Myrkovir Forest. Papa grunted and stormed back to the house, stomping up the steps where we sat.

"Quit your weepin' and get to your chores," he grumbled as he passed us and slammed the door behind him.

I flinched in Tessa's arms. She kept stroking my hair as we both continued to cry, watching Mama grow smaller and smaller until she disappeared around a bend.

"Don't you worry, Mur. She'll come back," my sister promised. "Mama will come back."

But she never did.

CHAPTER 1

Sixteen Years Later

MURGHA

THE SPRITE WAS BACK. SHE WAS SITTING ON AN UPPER SHELF NEAR THE door where Papa had lined up several metal tankards—the ones he commissioned from the blacksmith to sell to travelers.

She was a wood sprite, no taller than my hand from the heel of my palm to the tip of my middle finger. She was quite pretty.

Her tiny female body was the vibrant blue of a summer sky, covered in downy feathers up to and over her breasts, where her skin, a paler blue, covered her throat and face. Her slender legs ended in sharp black talons, which she currently used to perch on the lip of the shelf above me.

She stretched out her black-tipped wings and yawned, revealing tiny, serrated teeth. Wood sprites had bird-like wings instead of arms like other sprites. Her head was small and smooth and covered in tiny blue feathers that curled up at the back of the neck. And she watched me with large, round black eyes.

I continued to sweep, trying to ignore the game of Kings and Bones Papa had been playing with customers for the past three hours. I wondered why she was watching me.

She'd first appeared not long after we settled here in these woods. Our high lord had been moving us frequently the past several years as the war between Northgall and Lumeria became more volatile. We'd settled here north of the Borderlands last winter in the dense forest not too far from Lake Moreen. And since the ambassador now sitting at the table with my father had carried the news to us that the war was over—had been over for months, actually—it seemed we'd be staying here.

I didn't like it. We were currently living on Northgall lands. And while our high lord had assured us we were too far away from any of the dark fae to be in danger, I knew for a fact he was wrong.

My sister, Tessa, had been taken by one this past summer. Papa had been gravely ill, burning up with fever. She'd left in the middle of the night to fetch juniper to help with the fever, and she'd never returned.

The next morning, I found a letter attached to something small wrapped in fine leather on our doorstep. The letter bore my name in Tessa's hand. Though it was certainly her penmanship, I was sure she was forced to write the letter, telling me she'd met a beast fae, who was now her mate.

That was ridiculous! We'd spoken that very night about how awful and terrifying the dark fae were. She'd never simply galivant off and leave me to mate with one.

In the letter, Tessa had asked me to meet her that night at the stream if I wanted to go and live with their clan instead of stay with Papa.

Nonsense. As if I'd fall for that. The beast fae who'd captured her had obviously forced her to write the letter to try to lure me away from home and the protection of our wood fae clan.

I didn't fall for it, of course.

However, I did find a beautifully made dagger and scabbard wrapped inside the leather. Tessa's letter had said it was a gift for my protection. It made me wonder about a captor who would allow her to send me a gift before spiriting her away in the middle of the night.

The dagger was small and fit perfectly in my hand. From that day on, I strapped the dagger to my thigh beneath my homespun dress. Without Tessa at my side, I felt even more vulnerable and would have to protect myself.

The wood sprite walked behind several tankards and settled right above my father and the men playing Kings and Bones like she was actually interested in the game. Curious.

I'd noticed her while I was gathering fennel in the woods last summer, not long before Tessa was taken. She'd followed me home that afternoon. When I called up to her in the branches, she said not a word, but simply watched me. All sprites could speak, but I wondered if she couldn't since she never did.

She reappeared many times over the next several months, simply observing me as I hung the laundry to dry behind our inn or worked in the small garden out back. She even followed me from tree to tree when I went in search of herbs in the woods.

Since Tessa left, I found the wood sprite's company comforting, even if she never spoke to me. She still felt like a friend.

"More mead, Murgha!" bellowed Papa from the corner table, his words slurring.

The sun was slanting through the western window, casting shadows on the rough wood plank floor.

There was no one else in the tavern of our four-room inn built beneath a giant black oak tree. The only customers were the three men at the table with Papa—the moon fae ambassador from Mevia and his two guardsmen.

"Hurry, girl," Papa called, rattling the bits of stone and bone in the pewter bowl before scattering them on the board of kingdoms carved into the table.

"Well done, Phestys," said the ambassador. "Seems you're on a winning streak."

My gut clenched as I retrieved a pitcher of mead from behind the bar and made my way to their table. Papa had always been a gambler. Even worse since Tessa left.

Once his fever had broken last summer, he'd stormed to the high lord's council and demanded they go after the creature who'd stolen his daughter. But our high lord was a useless coward.

Even though it was his idea to leave our home in Myrkovir Forest and flee to a *safer* place away from the war, he was the one who rarely stayed in residence here. He was always leaving for some important summit in Morodon on the coast or somewhere far away.

Ironically, he'd taken us here for safety, and yet, Tessa had been stolen in the night. Simply vanished into thin air.

"So I am, my lord," agreed Papa with a belchy chuckle, hauling his coin closer.

I poured him more mead then moved to the ambassador, a noble-born Mevian by the name of Rukard. Though I felt his eyes on me, I refused to look at him as I refilled his cup.

He was about Papa's age, some gray at his temples, his long brown hair tied back in a tail. His fancy Mevian silk garb threaded with silver embroidery signified his importance. While I stood next to him, he flared his indigo wings as if he was trying to impress me.

The moon fae were the only light fae who had beautiful, iridescent wings, ones that my true father would've had.

The ambassador's wings didn't impress me, nor did his lecherous stare. His two guardsmen both wore the blue and silver armor of Mevia. They were bulkier than the ambassador, of course, and their wings were a deep shade of blue.

I couldn't pretend their wings didn't fascinate me a little. Wood fae were considered a lower caste, not as anointed by the gods to be given the gift of wings.

Yet, I was well aware that the color of my white-blond hair and violet eyes set me apart from other wood fae. Only the noble line of Issosian moon fae had the same coloring of hair and eyes as me. Except they also were all born with wings. I was not. I was a half-breed.

"Why don't we up the stakes, Phestys?"

I glared at Rukard while I filled the bigger guard's cup first. Rukard grinned at me, but his eyes kept wandering lower.

"I've got the pot now," said Papa haughtily. "I'll set the wager, my lord."

I set the black-haired guard's cup down, ignoring his sly wink at me then rounded him to place a hand gently on my father's shoulder. "Papa, you've done so well. You should stash that away for good keeping. The winter will be here—"

"Oh, go on with you, Murgha." He shoved me aside. "Go clean the tables from the customers."

I didn't bother telling him they were all clean because we'd had no customers since the ambassador and his men had arrived two days ago.

Wood fae didn't much like the company of moon fae. It

wasn't that we were enemies, but moon fae would often throw their weight around, especially ones with the authority of a noble lord like Rukard. They made other fae nervous.

As they were making me right that very minute.

On the table, the kingdoms were carved into four squares around a circular center. Each of the squares represented four realms—the heavens marked with stars, the oceans marked with wavy lines, the earth marked with round stones, and the mountains marked with spiky peaks. At the center of them all was the circle of the three hells, divided into pie-shape triangles. And at the very center of the triangles was a throne.

When a player cast the pewter bowl filled with three stones, six leg bones and the skull of a rodent, wherever they landed determined the roller's points for that round. I never bothered to learn the exact rules because I detested the game so much.

It seduced Papa into gambling away good money we needed to keep food in the larder and mead in our barrels. Not only for us but for our customers.

What I did know was that stones held more points than bones. The four realms on the outside were the safest and gave more points than the three hells. But anything landing on the throne doubled the points earned in that roll. And if the rodent skull landed on the throne, the roller was declared the winner no matter what anyone else rolled in the round.

Papa shoved every last coin he had into the empty square at the left of the table where the bets were made. "Everything in," he chuckled.

A stone of dread sank to the pit of my stomach. I'd seen this before, my father's unwavering optimism in conquering a player when it usually was the other way around.

"That's mighty steep." Rukard said with a serious expression while he scratched his clean-shaven chin thoughtfully. "But I'll take the wager."

He pulled from the inside pocket of his fine, embroidered jacket a leather satchel of coin that he upended onto the pile. It wasn't just silver and copper pieces but the definitive sparkle of gold in the mix.

I gasped. So did Papa. But not for the same reason. While Papa's eyes gleamed greedily, I knew that mine shone with fear.

"I'll add this as well," quipped Rukard, pulling a gold ring encrusted with a trio of sapphires from his finger and laying it on top of the coin with a heavy clink.

"I'm out," said the dark-haired guardsmen.

"Me too," added the other, leaning back and drinking his mead.

"How about you, Phestys?" asked Rukard. "Surely, you can stay in the game, a man of your resources."

My stomach soured even more. Rukard knew exactly what to say to prick my father's pride and urge him further on.

"I...uh..." Papa faltered on a nervous chuckle. "I don't know if I can meet your wager."

He glanced up at me where I'd frozen a few feet away with the pitcher of mead in hand before he pulled something small that sparkled from his trousers' pocket and lay it next to the ring on the pile.

My free hand went instantly to my neck, even though I knew it wasn't there. It was my necklace, the one treasure I had from my mother. She'd left it behind when she left us. When I was ten, I'd taken it from Papa's box of trinkets and wore it from that day on.

Even though Papa had never given it to me, he saw that I had it and had never ordered me to give it back. When Tessa noticed, she simply said, 'It looks pretty on you.' And that was that.

Until about three months ago when it went missing. I'd thought maybe the chain had broken when I was working. I'd looked everywhere and had even asked Papa. He'd grumbled something about getting on with my chores.

But, apparently, he'd stolen it. It happened about the same time when Papa's drinking and gambling had begun to spin out of control, carrying us closer and closer to the brink of ruin. I wondered if he'd already used it to gamble once and had won it back.

Rukard reached over and lifted the delicate silver chain, holding the moonstone in his palm. I wanted to reach over and jerk it from his nasty grasp.

"Well, well. This is quite the beauty. Delicate and lovely to be sure." He tsked. "But if you want to meet my wager, you'll have to come up with something more."

"That's all I've got, my lord." Papa swiped a palm through his sweat-slick hair, and for a moment, I felt relief. He was going to give up.

But then Rukard's gaze cut to me. An icy finger of dread trickled down my spine. "I believe you do have something of great value, Phestys."

Papa's gaze followed his. All four men were staring at me. I couldn't imagine what my expression reflected. I felt frozen in utter fear that Papa would even consider it. And yet, I knew he would.

He'd only ever tolerated my presence, giving what affection he did have to Tessa. I was simply a servant in his house, another mouth to feed, but one who could earn her keep. Since Tessa left, it had become worse—his moods and his sour grumbling about the sad lot fate had dealt him as he sank further into his cups and into gambling.

"Papa..." I begged softly without saying anything more than his name.

He averted his gaze to the pile of sparkling coin and the sapphire on top. "Aye. My daughter Murgha would even the scales."

"Indeed," agreed Rukard with a lascivious grin before turning back to the game.

A flicker of blue caught my eye as the wood sprite zipped out the open window. A sense of doom weighed even heavier. It was like she'd sensed the coming shame and loss, for I was certain that Rukard didn't want me as a servant to sweep his floors and clean his kitchen.

A round in the game of Kings and Bones consisted of each player rolling three times, the one with the highest total points winning the game. So I had the time it would take for six rolls to sneak my way through the kitchen to the residential part of the house where I could flee out the back.

Trembling, I rounded the bar to wash the now empty pitcher. I rinsed it quickly and set it on a towel to dry. *Rattle, rattle, swish.*

Papa rolled his first one. "Haha!" He laughed. "The finest roll yet," he declared with glee.

"Quite so," said Rukard, not seeming ruffled.

I kept my head down, pretending to clean items with trembling hands as I made my way closer to the swinging door that led into the kitchen.

"That was eighteen points on that one, my lord. Your roll."

Rattle, rattle, swish.

"Not bad, not bad," said Papa, a twinge of nervousness in his voice.

I kept wiping the towel down the bar then tossed it on a barrel before stepping toward the kitchen door.

A strong hand caught my arm and tugged me back. I gasped and looked over my shoulder at the dark-haired guard.

"Why don't you come and watch the game, Murgha?" he said too familiarly.

I didn't even know his name, nor had I ever introduced myself, yet the smug quirk on his mouth told me he wasn't asking. He was telling me what to do.

"I should clean up after a long day," I told him.

"No," he declared, "you should come watch your new master win you to his house."

My belly rolled with nausea again. I wondered how much longer before I'd empty my stomach onto the floor.

I didn't resist because there was no use, but he hauled me back to the table roughly and forced me down onto a stool next to him at the bar. He let go of my arm, but his close proximity was a warning that he could snatch me if I tried to get away.

I clasped my hands in my lap, grazing the strap at my thigh that held my dagger beneath my dress. Relieved that I had that for protection at least, I blew out a shaky breath.

By the time they'd ended the second round, Rukard was up by five points. Papa didn't seem dismayed. Like I'd said, he was an optimist in the throes of gambling. He always thought he'd win... until he didn't.

My entire body was shaking by the time Papa scooped the bones and stones into the pewter cup and began to shake them for his final roll.

Rattle, rattle—

The tavern door slammed open, knocking the wall behind it with a shudder. Everyone jumped, but the guard at my side was on his feet, his sword unsheathed. Then, no one moved at all.

We were all frozen at the sight standing in the doorway, the setting sun silhouetting a giant shadow fae—one of demonkind

—in all of his terrifying glory. His wide dragon-like wings blocked out nearly all of the light, his four horns curled back in an elegant crown over his sleek black hair.

Then he dipped his head and folded his wings tightly against his back so he could walk through the doorway made for light fae, not for the oversized demonkind.

The guard at my side stepped forward with more bravado than I thought he had and demanded, "State your purpose here, shadow fae. This inn does not accommodate the likes of you."

The shadow fae stepped across the room, his heavy boots sounding hard on the wood floor. The newcomer stopped next to the table where Papa and Rukard were also staring in shock up at him. The dark fae's red-eyed gaze flickered to each one of them, stopping on me for a lingering moment before returning his attention to the table, not to the guard who'd spoken to him.

"I am a shadow fae priest," he stated in a deep, silken voice, "and I have come to play the game."

CHAPTER 2

MURGHA

At first, no one said a word. I'd heard of the shadow fae priests but knew only enough that if I encountered one, I should run fast in the other direction. They were the elite warriors of the shadow fae clans who lived in a city called Gadlizel high in the Solgavia Mountains. They were brutal and deadly and should not be trifled with.

Even so, the guard at my side decided that he would. He was either very stupid or very brave. Perhaps a bit of both.

"We don't want your kind here," said the guard. "You should leave."

I'd expected the shadow fae to scowl with indignation, perhaps snap a few words about insolence and disrespect. However, the towering shadow fae did none of that. He merely arched one dark brow, his mouth quirking with what seemed amusement.

Again, he disregarded the guardsman, completely ignored him, and addressed Papa and Rukard, "I'm joining the game."

This time, the silkiness in his voice was laced with warning.

"There's only one roll left," protested Rukard.

Papa was smart enough not to talk back to the lethal-looking stranger.

"Then you have a greater chance to win," said the shadow fae. He placed two things on the table—first, an unsheathed black-steel blade about as long as my arm from shoulder to elbow, and second, a pouch of coin, twice as large as Rukard's.

Papa's smile finally appeared as he stared at the mound of coin that was fortune enough to last a lifetime.

"My roll," said my father, gathering the stones and bones into the cup.

I hadn't moved an inch since the stranger had appeared in the doorway. I suddenly realized my pulse throbbed in my throat, my heart rate speeding wildly.

Both guards had taken vigil behind Rukard, arms crossed and expressions grim. But my attention was entirely on the stranger.

I'd met a few wraith fae before, on my visits to the Border-lands, but I'd never seen a shadow fae this close. Only from a distance that one time.

On a late afternoon last winter, Tessa and I had been foraging in the woods for whatever we could find before the first snow.

"Look, Mur! Up there!" she'd shouted excitedly.

I followed where she pointed. "I don't see anything."

"By that tall mountain, don't you see them? Shadow fae."

And then I did. They were quite far away, thankfully, since Tessa was shouting loud enough to wake the dead. I watched the three dark fae creatures flying in a triangular line until they disappeared over the peak.

"Good thing they stay in their mountains," I observed.

"Indeed." Then we went back to foraging.

That had me wondering even more about the stranger. We'd been told by countless fae who lived in the area they didn't often come down from their mountains. So why was he here, playing a game of Kings and Bones with the likes of my father and the ambassador?

I observed the stranger at my leisure, realizing something I hadn't noticed at first because my attention was entirely drawn to his horns and wings and giant presence. He was strikingly beautiful.

His eyes were a shocking shade of crimson, and his face was carved into sharp, lovely lines at the cheeks and jaw, his mouth full and wide.

His intense gaze was on the game as Papa rolled, but it flicked to me long enough to make sweat bead down my back. I looked at the game to avoid his gaze.

"How about that?" Papa laughed heartily, tallying his points aloud. "That's fifty-six you'll have to beat."

Though I didn't play the game, I knew it was a high number.

Rukard took the cup and rattled it for his final roll. When he spilled the contents of the cup, I noted his wicked smile spread wide. I also noticed the fall of my father's face. Though he'd never loved me as his own daughter and though I'd warned him countless times about his gambling, particularly this afternoon, I couldn't help feeling pity for him.

"Seems I'm in the lead now," said Rukard, sliding his smile to me.

I winced, realizing I could very well be leaving with this foul man. I let my hand rest on top of the dagger beneath my dress, taking comfort. I'd slice his face off, or something worse, if he tried to touch me.

I could search for Tessa. Perhaps, the beast fae who'd taken her was actually caring for her in his clan. It was my only option other than finding work in the Borderlands. But a young female alone was a prime target for all manner of crime.

The shadow fae reached his clawed hand across the table and scooped up the bones and stones into the cup. He rattled them once then flung them across the table.

Papa gasped. I couldn't see properly from where I was sitting so I stood and stepped to the side, directly facing the stranger now. But I was staring at the board where the rodent skull sat perfectly at the center of the throne on the board.

I looked at the shadow fae who was staring at me, his expression hard, unyielding, and a glint of determination in his demon gaze.

"No," declared Rukard. "You cheated. You used your magick to make that happen."

For a moment, the shadow fae didn't even acknowledge him, his gaze entirely on me. Then he blinked slowly and rose from the table, turning his attention to the blustering ambassador.

He replied with nothing more than a cold glare. Then he reached across the table and scooped up his pouch of coin, not bothering with the rest, and gripped his black-steel blade on the table. "Get your things, female."

How did he know I had been wagered in this game? He'd entered the inn after the wager.

My mind spun at the prospect of leaving the only home I'd ever known—albeit a sad one lately—and going with this fearsome shadow fae.

"*Now*," he clipped, his command jerking me into motion.

Instantly, I stalked away from the men, the tension mounting in the room. Perhaps they'd start fighting while I was gone gathering my things, then I could slip away. But as I crossed through the kitchen and into our private part of the house, I heard the distinct sound of heavy boots following me.

CHAPTER 3

VALLON

She wasn't what I imagined she'd be. The problem was I'd been thinking of her as a small child. My search for her using Gwendazelle had been fruitless for so many months. Who knew the half-breed fae would move right into dark fae territory so close to my own home?

It was the gods' doing. They'd wanted me to find her.

I followed her scent through the small tavern and house since she'd practically run from the room. She'd try to run again, I was certain.

Just as I knew that ambassador and his guards would attack me once we left here. This was a small clan of wood fae. I'd discovered their lord had moved them here to avoid the war, and since the war was over, I'd thought he would have moved them back to their homeland in Lumeria. No matter the wraith king now occupied both Northgall and Lumeria, they'd have likely been more at ease back in their own part of the world.

Murgha was certainly not safe here. She stood out, not just as a light fae who didn't belong in the dark fae realm, but as a half-breed moon and wood fae who didn't fit in among her own kind. Not one wood fae had hair and eyes like hers.

That's because it was a trait only passed down in the noble line of the moon fae, pure bloods believed to be descended from the Moon Goddess Lumera herself. And Murgha most definitely carried that blood in her veins.

Winding through the residence, I stepped into her bedchamber, smaller than the closet for my armor and weapons back in the Solgavia Mountains. Her nervous gaze flicked to mine, but she continued to pack the clothes from the small trunk at the foot of her bed into a cloth satchel. She kept silent but watchful while I remained at the doorway.

After she'd emptied whatever was in the trunk, she cinched the rope of the small pack and turned to me, lifting her chin defiantly. She didn't question who I was, why I'd come, or where I was taking her. She simply looped a shabby green cloak around her shoulders, buckled the clasp, and waited.

Puzzled, I nodded at the door. "Come."

Then I turned and exited through the back door rather than going through the tavern. I heard her light footsteps following. Otherwise, I would've spun around and lifted her over my shoulder to take her from this place.

As it was, I should've come sooner. There was a bluish tinge beneath her eyes and she was far too thin. She wasn't being cared for properly by that worthless father of hers. Who wasn't her father at all.

But I'd been too distracted by what was happening in Gadlizel. By serving my prince, I'd been neglecting my oath to my own father. My gut clenched at the sourness of it.

What if I hadn't been stationed a few, short leagues from here? What if Gwenda hadn't brought me the message in time that the innkeeper was gambling away his daughter to a lascivious piece of filth from Mevia?

When we stepped outside, I swept the area but found no sign of the ambassador and his guards. Not even the girl's reprobate of a father. Nor did I see any wood fae coming to protest that a demon fae was stealing away with one of their clanswomen.

I snorted at the indignity of it. They'd let me take her with not even the smallest objection or struggle.

Above us, we were shrouded by a thick canopy of black oak trees. The branches were too thick and would likely scrape the female if I tried to fly straight out of here. It wouldn't bother me in my armor, but her dress was threadbare, and the cloak she wore was no better. I'd have to find some better clothing for her before we reached Solgavia.

The clearing where I'd landed and had come into the village was only a little ways through the woods. We could lift off from there.

"This way, female," I called over my shoulder.

She scowled, but followed me, which for some reason made me smile. Anger burned hotly beneath that glower of hers, her thumping heartbeat a sweet, tantalizing thrum in the air. My canines ached at the thought of tasting her.

That was unusual. Startling, even. Especially when I let my mind wander to its deeper meaning. But that couldn't be so.

Shaking it off, I commanded, "Walk beside me. There may be brigands in the forest ahead."

I hated traveling by foot. There were all manner of opportunists in these dense woods far from civilization, waiting to rob or do worse to travelers.

"The only brigand I see is walking in front of me." Her voice was sweet as pure honey, but her words were laced with poison.

Yet again, I fought a smile. She was feisty, the little moon fae.

"I'm no cutthroat, Murgha, but I will cut a throat when necessary."

She went quiet after that. I should try to put her at ease rather than frighten her, but fear was a good motivator. And until we were far from her village, I needed to keep her moving by whatever means necessary.

The last light of dusk filtered through the trees at an angle. I glanced up at the flash of blue of Gwenda zipping overhead.

"How do you know my name?" came the quiet question behind me.

I stopped and turned to face her. She froze on the path, not moving any closer but not stepping back either when I erased the short space between us.

"That's what you want to know?" Of all the things she could ask me, I was somehow surprised that was the first.

"I don't know you," she declared with her chin tilted up, though she couldn't keep her voice from trembling, "but you know my name."

That was a story I couldn't tell her here. "We're almost to the clearing. We need to keep moving."

Suddenly, Gwenda chirped a high trill from the branches above, giving me a second's notice before they fell on me. I shoved Murgha to the side and whipped around, blade swiping through the air.

My short-sword sliced into the moon fae's shoulder. He cried out and dropped the serrated knife he'd been about to bury into my back, his dark blue wings flapping and pulling him out of reach.

Instantly, I ducked, sensing another one diving at me on the right. He missed my neck but slashed across my left wing, the pain sharp. Growling, I stabbed straight into his throat, my sharp black steel burying deep. His eyes went round in shock that his life was over so quickly.

"You should've let it go," I advised him before I yanked my short-sword free and gave him a shove.

He fell backward, crimson blood instantly soaking the grassy path. When I turned, the other guard was still groaning on the ground, holding his bleeding arm.

Striding to him, I stepped on his wing to get his attention and pointed the tip of my blade at his throat.

He froze, staring up at me, hatred in his gaze. "You cheated, you fucking bastard."

He was right. "It doesn't matter," I said casually. "The female is mine regardless."

A sharp twinge twisted in my chest at the truth of the words. I hadn't meant them in the way her father, and even that ambassador, thought of her as their property. I'd meant she was mine to protect. By a solemn vow I would not break. Not for anyone. Still, the possessiveness of the words rang true, burrowing deeper, etching into my very bones.

"Don't try to follow us. I won't be so forgiving the next time," I promised him, then nicked his chin for good measure. He flinched and whimpered but still didn't move as the trickle of red trailed down his throat.

Certain that I'd made my point, I looked back toward the village. No one else was coming to fetch the half-breed moon fae who'd been gambled away by her father like a piece of copper. It was sickening. And these two guards had only come to try to win back their honor since they realized I'd tricked them.

Re-sheathing my blade, I turned to find that Murgha wasn't waiting close by. She wasn't anywhere. Huffing, I nearly laughed.

Of course, she'd run. I strode down the path toward her scent —a mixture of lemon, lavender, and spice. It lingered in the air, a teasing aroma that yet again made my canines ache.

My desire was unexpected, and yet the burning heat of want curled hotly inside me all the same. A growl rumbled in my chest before I beat my wings and flew after her beneath the high branches, seeking my prey.

CHAPTER 4

MURGHA

I pumped my legs as fast as they would go, my lungs burning from the exhausting run. My skirt didn't even hinder me as I flew through the darkening woods. I'd left the path and was sure I could find some dense brush deep enough in the forest to hide until night came. Then I could find my way back home.

I remembered there was a particularly thick bramble of berries this way. If I could only make it there, I'd slip inside and remain quiet as a hare until he was gone.

Then I heard it. I'd never actually heard the exact sound before, the beating of very large wings, but I knew what it was all the same.

I whimpered as the sound drew closer. I didn't dare look over my shoulder, knowing what I'd find.

Suddenly, strong arms were around my waist, lifting me off the ground.

"No!" I screamed, kicking out wildly with my legs and clawing at his forearm, which had me scraping uselessly at his steel vambrace.

He landed with a thud beneath a thick-trunked tree, squeezing me so tight my breath whooshed out of my chest.

"Easy, Murgha," he whispered close to my ear, the silky caress of his voice raising gooseflesh on my skin. "Calm down."

My heart thought that was a ridiculous idea. It only beat faster, now that I was trapped in the arms of the shadow fae priest. I feared what he planned to do with me. If it was anything like the ambassador had surely been planning for me, I wasn't going to allow it without a fight.

I stopped struggling, realizing it was pointless. My breath heaved in and out of my chest, my pulse still racing. I'd have to plan my escape another way.

"There now," he said in that soothing tone that only made me angrier.

"How do you know my name?" I asked again, slowly inching my skirt up my leg with the tips of my fingers.

"We're not out of danger yet, and I need to get you safely out of these woods before we have that conversation."

"Safely?" I scoffed. "You have your arms so tight around me I can't breathe."

He eased his hold but still kept me pressed close. It allowed me to pull my skirt up higher so that I could finally reach the scabbard strapped to my thigh.

I tried to ignore the way his hard, warm body felt pressed against my back, the way he smelled so pleasant like clean, fresh air and cedarwood.

"You're also holding me against my will," I snapped. "I'd say *you're* the danger."

He chuckled lightly, the rumble vibrating to my back then he dipped his head close to my ear again. "Perhaps you're right," he crooned in that velvet voice. "Maybe you should be a good girl and not run off."

Then he released me from his hold. I spun around at the same time, whipping the dagger from its scabbard. If he was surprised, he didn't show it. Actually, his gaze wasn't even on the blade I held but on my leg.

When I glanced down, I realized that the hem of my skirt and chemise had caught on the scabbard, revealing far too much of my pale thigh. I jerked the skirts free and dropped them, then pointed the dagger at him more threateningly, narrowing my gaze. "Don't come near me."

His red eyes gleamed with pleasure as if I'd said something sweet and alluring. Then he stepped closer, doing exactly what I warned him not to do.

"I'm serious, you demon," I spat, my dagger digging into his jaw. He seemed not to care at all. "Don't come a step closer."

He didn't, but he did, however, reach out his hand and lift a strand of my long hair.

"So soft and pretty," he murmured, "like silver silk."

I grabbed his wrist with my free hand and pressed the blade to the skin of his throat. His arrogant smile spread wide, the strands of my hair sliding through his fingers. I shivered at the sensation, not understanding why it both disturbed and thrilled me.

"Don't test me," I warned, injecting as much venom as I could into my voice. "I'll stab you right through the heart."

His scarlet gaze devoured me with fiery heat, but the timbre of his voice remained steady and cool. "My sweet, of that I am positively sure."

Puzzled, I frowned, then suddenly he snatched the blade from my hand, scooped me up, sprinted three steps, and beat his great black wings, lifting us into the air. I squealed as he aimed for a narrow opening between branches. He curled an arm over my head as he pummeled right through, breaking through with a snap of branches. We were airborne.

For a moment, I squeezed my eyes shut, not even caring that I clung to him like a frightened kitten. I'd clawed one hand into the back of his leather doublet, the other into his chest. He didn't seem to mind at all, soaring through the sky without a care.

Soaring. I forced my eyes open and turned my head to look. I gasped. We weren't far above the tree line, heading northwest. The sun had dipped behind the Solgavia Mountains in the distance, the sky a swath of indigo with the first twinkling of stars.

Up here, everything seemed so ethereal and illusory. The sky, the mountains, the trees and the ground below. They were all real, and yet, when gliding between the earth and stars, the world felt more like a dream, one that appealed to me far more than reality.

For the first time in my life, I felt a pang of grief that I hadn't been born with wings. From the day my mother left, the same day I had realized my white hair and purple eyes signified not only that I was different but my birth was repellant, I'd wished I had dark hair and warm, brown eyes like my sister, Tessa. Like my mother. I'd only ever wanted to belong to them.

But now, flying high above the world, I wanted to be more like my father. Instead, I was cursed to be neither wood fae nor moon fae, floating somewhere in between.

"What are you thinking?" His deep voice jarred me.

I stared out at the glowing horizon, the sun kissing the sky one last time before he slept.

"I was thinking how apt that I should love this so much. Flying."

When I didn't expound, he asked, "Why is it so fitting?"

"Because here, you're between two realms, the heavens and the earth. That's always been me. Caught between two worlds, never belonging to either."

He said nothing, beating his wings once, gliding lower as we passed over the thick woodland.

"I wish I could stay here," I murmured to myself.

He shifted me in his hold. It seemed he wanted to look at me, meet my gaze.

"I'll bring you any time you like, Murgha."

My brow pinched at my name as I was reminded this shadow fae priest somehow knew me. That disconcerting sensation returned. "How do you know who I am?"

Rather than avoid me yet again, he answered in a somber tone, "I'll tell you everything after we get settled for the night."

Then he aimed for a grove of giant black oak trees, taking us back to earth.

CHAPTER 5

VALLON

I LOWERED US VERTICALLY THROUGH THE TOP BRANCHES OF THE OLD OAK I'd made my home these past few months. I'd trimmed only a few of the thicker ones so that I could come and go easily enough and see the stars when I fell asleep.

From down below, no one would ever suspect there was a fae aerie stretching across one side of the tree. We were too far up and too many leaf-covered branches hid my makeshift camp.

I set Murgha on her feet and her small bag next to her. I'd scooped it up off the forest floor along with her when I was finally done arguing. Truthfully, I needed to cool off, and going airborne was the best way to find inner balance.

Murgha unsettled me, and not for the reasons I'd taken her away from that so-called father.

She instantly backed away, gripping a branch for support. The thick, leafy branches cradled my pallet, almost like a nest. The pallet was bare except for the layers of furs that was my bed near the trunk and the satchel I had hanging on the end of a broken branch that acted like a hook.

She stared, wide-eyed, her pulse beginning to beat faster again. Strange, the flight in the sky had calmed her when I knew it had been her first time in the air. It was only when the reality that she was in the hands of a stranger had settled in that her fear had returned.

I lifted one of the deerskin hides and spread it out on the other side of the pallet near her. "Have a seat."

She remained very still, staring at me warily.

"I won't hurt you, Murgha."

She held my gaze for a moment longer, then seemed to believe me. For the moment, at least.

After opening my satchel, I pulled out a portable fire-pit. With a twist at the bottom, the bowl opened up like flower petals, sealing into place. I set it on the flat stones beneath the opening in the branches. The stones kept the pallet from catching fire. Then I found the blue-coal in my satchel that I'd managed to barter from some wraith fae at the Borderlands.

"You have blue coal?" she asked curiously, knowing what it was as I lit them with a match and dropped three coals into the metal pit.

"You've seen it before?" I asked.

She shook her head and scooted closer to peer into the bowl, reaching out her palms to feel the heat. A small smile lifted her mouth and brightened her face.

I rubbed at my sternum.

"My sister, Tessa, and I heard about it from one of our clansmen after he'd gone traveling to the Borderlands." She peered even closer. "It really doesn't give off any smoke?"

"No."

"But how?" she asked, seeming both fascinated and disbelieving.

I couldn't help but smile at her keen curiosity. "Something about the properties of Vixet Krone make it the perfect element to provide warmth while never producing smoke. Just like the black steel that comes from there as well. It is the strongest metal on earth." I unbuckled my belt and set my blade aside.

"Vix's magick then."

"Mm," I agreed wordlessly.

"Why was Vixet Krone so special?" she asked.

Watching the blue light from the coal-fire gild her soft features, I shifted to wrap my arms at my knees, flaring my wings for balance. Her gaze skimmed over my wings then returned to me.

"Vixet Krone was once a volcano that covered a vast territory of Northgall. Legends say the god Vix lived beneath it with his mate, Mizrah."

"I've heard of her. That's what they call the wraith king's concubine, is it not?"

"Past wraith kings, yes." I remembered that last meeting with the new wraith king and that look in his gaze he set upon his Mizrah Una. "However, King Gollaya has become a different kind of wraith king."

"Really?" Her brow raised in surprise. "The ambassador had only brought us news that the war was over and how our people were faring back in Lumeria."

It figured he wouldn't bother to tell them the more important news, that King Goll was changing the world of both the light and the dark fae with his new regime.

"Tell me more about the volcano," she urged.

"When Mizrah died, it was said he was filled with such grief and torment that when he wailed and cried for her, it erupted the volcano where he'd once lived."

She watched as I unlaced the vambraces at my arms and the armor plates at my shoulders, setting the pieces aside. I didn't wear full armor, only the basics that were necessary when traveling outside of Gadlizel. We were enemies to everyone except other shadow fae, so it was always important to be on guard.

"And so the wraith fae built their home there."

"They did," I agreed.

"Why didn't the shadow fae and the beast fae? Why was it only the wraiths that claimed that place as their home?"

I huffed a laugh. "I don't know how that happened since it was thousands of years ago and never recorded by scribes. But beast fae are nomadic. They prefer to keep their clan moving throughout the year."

She seemed to think on that for a moment and then asked, "And what about you? The shadow fae?"

A strange thread of pleasure wound through me when she asked about my kind, even something as small as this.

"Shadow fae prefer to live up high. It's only natural that our home is in the mountains."

Her gaze returned to my wings, and then her brow pursed. "You're bleeding," she said on a gulp and pointed over my left shoulder.

When I looked, I could just see a trickle of blue from the cut the guard's sword had made. Rising, I went to my satchel again and removed a vial of antiseptic that our healers in Gadlizel made. I poured some on a clean cloth and stretched out my left wing.

I could barely reach the cut, but I could see that the guard's blade hadn't gone to the bone. Still, it was wide enough to cause infection.

"Damn," I muttered, reaching back to try and wipe the blue blood still streaming lightly from the wound.

"Let me."

I actually startled, finding Murgha standing right next to me. Without a word, I handed her the cloth.

"You'll need to sit down. I can't reach."

She was quite small, even for a light fae. I sat on the pallet and spread my wing. She stood eye level with the top of my wing. Then she dabbed at the cut, the sting of the medicine sharp, but I didn't move a muscle.

"This needs to be stitched," she said softly.

I looked up at her. "I don't suppose you know how to stitch wounds."

She swallowed nervously. "I do, actually. I sew all my own clothes, and Papa has needed cuts treated in the past. My sister was always too squeamish to do it."

"Would you stitch the wound for me?" I asked gently, wondering what she would do.

I could get Gwenda to do it. She'd been hiding in the upper branches watching us since we arrived. But I sincerely doubted she'd help me after I'd essentially abducted Murgha from her home. She was very fond of the fae female.

Murgha dabbed a few more times then asked, "Do you have a suture kit with you?"

My own pulse galloped a little faster. "It's in the front pocket of my bag."

She found it quickly and then returned to me. When she unwound the thread, she paused and observed it closely. "What kind of thread is this? It's much thicker than I'm used to."

"It's made in Gadlizel, specifically for wounds. The material we use comes from a plant called dellabore."

She threaded the needle and stepped close to my wing, her

fingers light and gentle as she pinched the skin close to make the first stitch. "I've never heard of dellabore."

"It only grows in the mountains."

"Not in fields, though," she stated, as if she knew for a fact. "Where does it grow exactly?"

She'd seemed to forget that I was the enemy, her curiosity about the plant getting the better of her. One thing Gwenda had reported the most about Murgha was her deep love of plants. She spent countless hours foraging in the woods and cultivating her own in a garden. I could probably get her full cooperation from now on by simply listing the properties of all of the exotic plants in Solgavia.

"Dellabore is a delicate shrub that grows in the lower elevation of the Solgavia Mountains. It cannot grow in the higher elevation where the temperatures are too cold. This time of year, it will be sprouting everywhere, especially near the streams that trickle through the foothills."

She continued stitching, but I could feel her burning to ask another question. I waited.

"What does it look like?"

Smiling to myself as she made another stitch, I replied. "The leaves are as big as your hand. The flowers have six spiky petals."

She paused to open her hand and looked at her palm.

"But it's the flower that's the most fascinating," I continued. "It blooms with thousands of tiny black thistles with a pink stamen at its center."

She tied off the stitch and leaned forward to bite the end, her warm breath coasting over my wing. I clamped my jaw tight and closed my eyes, forcing myself not to make a sound at the pleasure of it.

Most fae didn't realize that our wings were highly sensitive.

Though the skin was a tough hide, there was a sensitive web of nerves running just beneath.

"You use the thistles to create the thread?" she asked, walking to my bag and tucking the thread and needle back in the front pocket.

"Yes. It's a lengthy process of grinding the thistles with a binding mixture then flattening it thin before pulling it apart in tufts and spinning it into thread."

She returned to her place on the other side of the coal-fire and knelt on her knees, tucking her skirt around her. I frowned. She needed better clothes. Trousers, for one. Her legs would be exposed when we flew into colder climes.

"You know a lot about making thread. Is that one of the jobs of a shadow fae priest?" She blinked innocently but her eyes were mocking. She was teasing me? Another wave of warmth filled my chest.

"My mother was a spinner," I told her, not knowing why I wanted to share this with her, but I did. "That is what we call those who work on the looms creating dellabore thread and those who create the fabric from it."

Her eyes widened, her gaze flicking to my horns. "But you're a noble."

She understood that demon fae with four horns were noble-born.

"Was your mother common-born?" she asked.

I smiled. "In Gadlizel, there is no shame in work. Even the high-born work."

She seemed to want to say more but didn't.

"When I was small," I continued, "I'd sit at my mother's feet and play in the black tufts of dellabore, tossing them in the air."

"She wouldn't get angry?" she asked.

"No." I shook my head, smiling. "I was her only child, and she spoiled me."

Murgha smiled, and pleasure spread warmly through me.

"She made all my clothes, even this shirt." I tugged at the black sleeve.

She leaned forward but didn't ask to see it up close. Of course, she was still wary of me. She was an intelligent female and still had no idea why I'd taken her from that hovel of a home.

"Your mother? She is still living?" she asked tentatively.

"Very much. Strong as a Meer-wolf, she is." My smile softened. "But she doesn't spin or sew as much as she used to. Quite frankly, my father"—a twist of grief made me falter—"when he was alive, he fussed all the time that she should be relaxing and enjoying a life of leisure. But she would always tell him that sewing was what gave her the most enjoyment."

Murgha's violet eyes sparkled brightly by the coal-fire. "Your mother and father, they sound like very kind fae." She said this with a frown creasing her pretty brow.

She didn't understand why I'd taken her and what our connection was, but she was beginning to see I wasn't her enemy. I could never be.

As if she read my thoughts, she asked hesitantly, "Why did you take me from my home? How do you know who I am?"

I gave her a stiff nod then stood and whistled up to the boughs above us. "First, you need food."

Gwendazelle zipped down and settled on the leather strap of my satchel, blinking wide eyes at Murgha.

"It's you!" exclaimed Murgha, jumping to her feet.

Gwenda hid shyly behind a leafy twig, peaking her head out to watch Murgha.

"She's been watching me for months," said Murgha, her smile suddenly faltering. "She's your wood sprite? You sent her?"

"I don't own her." When I held out my palm, Gwenda instantly flew to me and curled her talons lightly around the edge of my hand. "She's my friend. And yes, I sent her to watch out for you. That's how I knew you were in trouble this afternoon."

Murgha blinked in surprise, not knowing what to say.

"Gwendazelle, this is Murgha." Gwenda opened a wing in greeting but Murgha simply stared in shock. "She will keep you company while I'm gone. I won't be long."

Gwenda flew off my palm and landed on a branch closer to Murgha. Knowing she couldn't run away from the top of this tree and that Gwenda would find and warn me if danger approached, I buckled my belt back on, sword at my hip, then flew up through the opening, the stars just beginning to shine.

CHAPTER 6

MURGHA

I sat back down cross-legged, tucking my skirt over my knees, and then stared at the wood sprite. I finally knew why she'd been following me for so many months. Well, sort of knew.

"Hi." I waved.

She lifted her wing again.

"Can you speak?" I asked.

"I speak," she said in a high-pitched voice.

I smiled. "You're very pretty."

She made a chirping trill sound, flew down to the wooden plank right in front of me, and said excitedly, "You're very pretty, too. And kind. I like you very much."

I laughed. "How do you know I'm kind?"

"You speak to the trees and flowers. They listen," she told me with deep sincerity in her round, black eyes. "I see you bring meals to the old fae lady who lives alone by the willow tree. I see you bring berries and nuts to the lame male who loves them but cannot walk far and find them himself."

I hadn't realized she'd watched me that much. I'd only seen her on occasion, mostly when I went into the woods.

My thoughts turned back to the shadow fae. "Why has he been making you follow me?" I pointed to the opening in the branches above us.

She shook her head. "He will tell you."

"What's his name?"

"Vallon."

His name soaked into my skin, and some tremble of awareness awoke inside me at hearing his name. A prickle of magick hummed quietly, as if waiting.

Waiting for what?

"He is a very important priest to the king." Then she added, "And the prince."

That only gave me more questions. "I just don't understand why a shadow fae I've never met, or even heard, of would have any interest in me."

"He will tell you," she repeated, blinking those large eyes sweetly.

So she wasn't going to give me any information about how or why I'd come to be here. Perhaps she'd tell me something else.

"How did you and Vallon become friends?"

Her smile widened to reveal a row of white serrated teeth. "That's a lovely story." She flew closer and perched on my knee, her talons pricking gently through my skirt. "Actually"—her pale blue brow scrunched into a frown—"it's a scary and sad story. Can I tell you a scary story?"

I nodded, instantly mesmerized before she said a word.

"My family and I lived in the woods at the foot of the Solgavia Mountains until we were hunted by evil creatures."

"What kind of creatures?"

"It was a flock of snow hawks."

"A flock?" I asked, puzzled. "But snow hawks are solitary birds."

And how could they be evil?

"Yes, they usually are." She bent her long legs and wrapped her blue wings around herself until only her tiny head peeked out. "But there was something wrong with them. My father and mother used their magick to try and stun them as they attacked." She shook her head. "But nothing could stop them. I was a mere nestling, but I saw them rip my father to pieces, and one of them carried my mother away in its sharp talons."

"I am so sorry." My heart ached for her, for I could see the pain etched in her face.

"I heard the cries of my siblings as I tried to fly away. We all flew from our nest in our home-tree, trying to hide in the woods. But one of the hawks caught me in his big claws." She sniffed, blinking her eyes sadly, but then her face brightened. "Suddenly, a giant shadow fae was there. He snatched the hawk by the throat and twisted its neck. It dropped me right into the fae's palm." She stood again and opened her wings. "The shadow fae was Vallon."

I had surmised that, but I didn't let on. "How fortunate he was there to save you."

"Yes, yes. He is my best friend." She made a sad chirping sound. "We couldn't find my siblings. They'd been taken away by the hawks. Vallon said there was a sickness inside of them since they didn't behave like regular hawks, and I agreed with him. Hawks don't prey on magickal creatures like wood sprites. But they weren't just sick. They were evil. I felt it, and I told him so."

I wondered at that. How could natural creatures be infected or tainted by some kind of evil? I'd never heard of such a thing.

"So you live with Vallon in Gadlizel?" I asked.

"Yes, yes. He is my family now."

Wood sprites typically lived in small families with other sprites. How curious, and even sweet, that Gwenda had attached herself to Vallon. But I suppose that would be natural if he saved her from certain death.

"You will like living in his villa. It is very beautiful."

I sat straighter suddenly, which had her puff out her feathers.

"Live with him?" My voice rose with shock. "Why on earth would I live with him?"

She blinked her dark eyes owlishly. "Because you are his to protect."

I laughed. "I don't even *know* him. By the gods, what in the world is going on?"

Then a flapping of giant wings raised my attention above me, his wingspan blocking out the stars as he lowered through the opening.

My breath caught as I took stock of him yet again. He was an extremely large male, his wings making him appear even more imposing. But it was the stark beauty of his face and his glittering red eyes that held me so captive and had my heart skittering faster as he landed on the far side of the coal-fire.

He carried an already skinned rabbit on a skewer and a bundle in his arms. His gaze swept over me as if he were looking for something, like he was ensuring himself I was still in one piece. Gwendazelle flitted to perch on the branch closest to the fire and cocooned herself into her feathers.

He settled the skewer crossways over the coal-fire. It fit perfectly into grooves on either side of the portable pit, obviously made for it.

"I've never seen such an efficient thing as that. Do the shadow fae make them?"

"No. They're a beast fae invention. Though the beast fae prefer natural fire over the blue coal."

"Why is that?" I asked.

He stepped around the fire and handed me the bundle of cloth. "The beast fae prefer the natural over magickal elements."

"What is this?" I stared down in my lap, seeing lacings. They were clothes.

"Those will suit you better and keep you warmer on our travels. I hope they fit. Change into them. I'll be back shortly."

Then with another whoosh, he was gone. Gwenda's eyes blinked sleepily, so I didn't bother her.

I unfolded the clothes in my lap. There was a pair of dark blue trousers made of a finer cloth than I'd had access to in our village. It was a thicker fabric, as was the beige blouse that laced in the front. There was also a black leather belt and a heavy coat.

Standing, I held out the coat that would hit my calves when I wore it. It was made of a deerskin pelt that had been smoothed into the softest leather, the color a pale brown, like cinnamon bark tea with the heavy cream I cherished whenever we could afford it.

We? There was no more "we," Papa and I. Tessa had been gone for almost a year, and it had felt less and less like home every season without her.

I'd always pretended that one day Papa would see me as his daughter and treat me as a cherished child, the way he had treated Tessa, his true-born daughter. But that had never happened. If I needed further proof of my worth to him, I only needed to remember that he had gambled me away like a piece of property.

I sniffed at the sting of it, blinking away the tears. I suppose it was only natural that a new life would garner me new clothes. Though I wasn't sure who this Vallon was, I was certain he had no intention of hurting me. Not only had he given me no reason to believe he would, but I sensed it with that inner whisper that sometimes spoke to me.

It didn't speak literally, but there had been moments when I simply knew something to be true. My magick, latent though it had been, would ripple along my skin and warm my body when it was trying to tell me something.

Gwenda said that I was under his protection. It was more than Papa had ever given me. So maybe this wasn't a terrible turn of events, but a new start. The thought of going back to the inn to Papa now made me nauseous.

Gwenda was now asleep, and I was sure Vallon had left me in privacy to change, so I stripped down to my shift, even removing the leather strap for my dagger, which was still missing. I was suddenly eager to put on these new clothes, to remove my old ones—my old life. When I picked up the shirt, an undergarment fell out.

It was made of the gossamer material of a chemise, though finer than my own. Removing my well-worn shift, I pulled the new one over my head. It had lacings at the bodice that tightened the chemise and held my breasts firmly in place. Not that mine were very big, but it felt good to have an undergarment that supported me there.

My old one was little more than a thin barrier so that I wouldn't chafe against the harsher wool dresses I owned.

My new chemise fell just past my hips. There were no other undergarments to wear beneath the trousers. When I pulled them on, they were of a thick material, but soft. I liked the feel of my new clothes as I added each layer.

When I saw my scabbard laying on the ground, I removed it from the leather strap and fitted it onto my new belt at my waist. When Vallon returned, I'd demand my dagger back.

By the time I pulled on the long coat, I was smiling and wishing I had a looking glass to see myself. The new clothes didn't only fit my body, they fit *me*. They made me feel stronger somehow, more confident.

The tell-tale flapping of giant wings warned me of his arrival. This time, I prepared for his overpowering presence.

When he landed, his gaze skated over me again, another inspection, but this time it was a slow perusal. When I glanced down at myself, I realized how well the clothes fit my petite figure and wondered where he'd gotten them.

"Where and how did you find clothes like this so fast? They fit perfectly."

"I see that," he drawled, standing very still as he continued to drink me in.

Heat flared in my cheeks. That was an expression I'd seen before on men. Many looked at me in such a way, some even offering gifts to seduce me. One traveler had outright offered coin for a night in my bed. But I'd avoided all of them, even the admirers I liked.

I was aware that as a half-breed, I wasn't an enticing catch as a wife. The males I'd admired in our clan never saw me that way.

The only time I'd ever let myself believe it was when Dellyn, the smithy's son, had started courting me. It was right after Tessa's disappearance, and so I'd gravitated toward his company and attention easily. I was lonely.

Dellyn had come to the inn often for that month, staying much longer after a meal and a pint of mead. We'd talked about our days, about the weather, about the war and hoping it would end.

One night, he'd left me a ring. It was fashioned from iron, not a precious metal, but it was intricately engraved with a vine of leaves. I remember that tender feeling that someone cared about me blooming in my chest.

I'd risen early the next morning before we opened the inn and tavern and gone to the blacksmith shop to thank him. I'd met with his father, who asked why I wanted to see his son. I remember the disapproving scowl he'd given me as I stood in his open doorway.

When I glanced down at the ring on my finger, the smithy seemed to realize what had happened. Perhaps he'd even seen his son forge it at their kiln because then he'd asked, "Did Dellyn give that to you?"

I was frozen, not knowing what to say, because his voice was harsh, angry, and obviously disapproving. Then Dellyn entered the room, and his father commanded darkly, "Whatever game you're playing, son, you best end it. *Now*."

That was when Dellyn took me outside, not angry with me but frustrated that I'd come to see him, to thank him. Because I was a green girl when it came to relationships with males, I'd asked him if he was courting me to be his wife.

Dellyn had flushed red and shook his head. "Not to be my wife. You know I could never take you as a wife. But I would be a good and kind lover to you, Murgha."

The way he'd offered to be my lover, like it was a gift, and then told me I could never be his wife, like the idea was preposterous, still tore me up inside to this day. That was when I realized I was a loathsome creature as a half-breed, an unwanted child born of a deceiving wife who cuckolded her husband. Perhaps they thought my mother's blood had tainted me to be the same sort of female. An unfaithful one. A female only good enough to warm their beds but never to let into their hearts.

I'd handed him his ring and walked back to the inn with my

head lifted and tears streaming down my cheeks. I'd never needed Tessa more than that moment.

But that day had taught me a fine lesson. That no matter what other males thought of me and the blood coursing through my half-breed veins, I was an honorable fae, and I would be a loyal wife if I ever found a male worthy of my love. So I guarded the one thing I could offer a true husband more preciously. I'd vowed not to give my virtue to any man but my husband.

Tessa had thought me silly since she'd had a few lovers and told me it was fun and pleasurable. But Tessa was a pure-blood wood fae. And men didn't look at her the way they did me. She couldn't understand why I was so wary of men.

So the shadow fae standing before me, giving my appearance a thorough and approving perusal, could look all his fill. Even if his heated gaze made warmth bloom beneath my skin with desire, I would not give him what he wanted.

"You know lots of small fae females you can snatch nice clothing from?" I asked.

That seemed to snap him out of his stupor. He settled back on his side of the coal-fire and turned the rabbit on its spit. The heat from the blue coal seemed to be cooking it quicker than a natural flame.

"I know a wraith fae female who lives in the Borderlands close by. She sold me the clothes."

"And you caught a hare as well in that short time? You're quite an efficient male."

His brow puckered uncomfortably, and a swath of pink climbed his neck. Was he actually blushing?

"She had been hunting so I bought the rabbit from her as well." He found my gaze across the coal-fire when I sat back down, cross-legged. "I thought you'd be hungry."

I was, but I had more important things to tend to than my stomach.

"Your name is Vallon." I nodded to the sleeping wood sprite. "Gwenda told me. What's your full name?"

His pause was brief then, "I am Lord Vallon of House Hennawyn, high priest of Gadlizel."

There was pride in his voice as he stated his name. As there should be. I knew by the four horns curling out of his head that he was a noble-born dark fae. And by the gold rings decorating them, I was aware he had high status.

Even so, hearing him say it made me understand why this shadow fae carried himself with such confidence and importance. He should be confident. Because he was important.

"And why has a high priest noble kidnapped a common-born wood fae?"

His gaze was sharp and assessing. This was the warrior I'd seen walk through Papa's tavern door.

Fierce yet cool, he held my gaze as he told me with unwavering certainty, "It was my father's dying wish. As well as yours."

CHAPTER 7

VALLON

Her violet eyes rounded in surprise, but she didn't say a word. What I had to tell her would come as a shock, and it would hurt her deeply. It was a sad story, and it was hers. I had to tell her for her to trust me at all.

"My father," I began, "loved to hunt. Have you heard of the black-horned mountain deer?"

She remained quiet but shook her head.

"It's a giant of a beast. Some grow as big as Pallasian stallions." And those horses could grow twice as tall as a dark fae. "They live high in the snow-capped mountains. And though we can easily fly up to hunt them there, it's rather difficult to carry them down the mountain. So we hunt them in the spring when they come lower for fresh grass."

I pulled the rabbit off the spit and tore a roasted leg off, handing it to Murgha. She took it, but her gaze remained fixed on me.

"Eat, Murgha."

"Tell me the story," she demanded.

"Eat," I repeated.

When she obeyed and nibbled on what I'd given her, the tightness in my chest eased. I pulled a piece off and ate while I continued.

"My father was hunting in the foothills when he heard men shouting and crying out, as well as the sound of a growling animal. He found four moon fae males fighting off a barga on a cliff. Well, three were fighting, and the fourth was injured."

Murgha gulped hard.

"You've heard of this bear then."

She nodded, brow pinched with concern. "When we were children, Papa would tell us to be good or the barga would get us."

"Not very kind of him."

"No."

"They're a fierce, territorial creature," I continued, "and when they're hungry, they will attack anything. They're four times my size, claws as long as your feet."

She glanced at her booted foot and tucked it tighter beneath her leg.

I ate the last bite of rabbit in my hand and pulled a rag and canteen from my bag. After wiping my fingers, I handed the canteen to her. She sipped it using one hand then handed it back. I settled back across from her.

"What happened next?" she asked.

"My father helped them fight the beast. He was an expert warrior and hunter. The barga finally realized it was outmatched and eventually ran off. One of the moon fae was an ambassador from Issos heading to the eastern realms with three guards. One of the guards who defended the ambassador against the barga had been mortally wounded."

My gut clenched, for this was the part I didn't want to tell her but knew I must.

"My father went to the moon fae, whose wing had been broken and his belly clawed open in the battle with the barga. There was no healer who could save him, my father knew. The injured male had the pale white hair and the purple eyes of a noble-born. He was an Issosian guard."

Murgha had abandoned her meal, the bit of rabbit hanging loosely in her hand in her lap. I should've had her finish her meal before I told her. Too late now.

"The Issosian guard reached out his hand to my father and pulled him close. He was dying. He told my father that he had failed his mate. She was a wood fae and married to another male. He'd found her too late, after she'd married and had a child with her husband, but she was now pregnant with his own child. While he knew he couldn't tear her from her family, he had promised he'd care for her always. He begged my father to watch over his child when he or she was born, knowing they'd be mistreated as a half-breed."

By now, Murgha's tears were streaming freely down her heart-shaped face, my insides twisting at the sight. But I had to tell her all of it.

"My father questioned why he didn't ask this of one of his own men. Why did he ask this of a shadow fae who lived far from the realm of the wood fae? But the Issosian guard knew that the vow of a shadow fae at someone's death was binding."

She didn't ask but a crease formed between her brow, so I explained.

"The shadow fae have a deep reverence for the dead and the

spirits when they go on into the afterworld. For us, a promise made to the dying is an eternal vow. Unbreakable."

I took a drink from the canteen then set it aside. "So my father promised to watch over the child when it was born, to be sure the babe was cared for. And he did for many years. He'd told me that she was a sweet little female, beloved by her mother and sister. And even when the man of her house threw the mother out, the girl was watched over by the sister and still provided for by the man, who was not truly her father."

She sobbed and dropped the leg of rabbit. I leaned across the space and handed her a handkerchief. She took it, sniffling softly, and wiped her face.

"My father told me all of this on his own deathbed just under a year ago, and he passed his vow onto me. Made me swear I would protect the female wherever she was in the world. For he'd lost track of her when her clan had left Myrkovir Forest to avoid the war. Then he became too ill to find her." That familiar well of knowing pulsed through my veins, that she—above all other duties and destinies—was the most important of them all. "To find you."

She sucked in a deep breath, wiping her face again, my heart aching to console her in some way. But I didn't move.

"And so," she began in a trembling voice, "the burden became yours to watch over me."

The pain in her voice and expression was as cutting as a sharp blade sliding deep. "Murgha"—I pulled her glassy gaze to mine —"it is not a burden for me."

If she knew what I'd realized in the past few hours, she'd likely want to run from me. But there was no return from the truth that had pounded itself into my flesh and bones the second I saw her standing in that tavern, awaiting her fate to be gambled away.

The thought of what her so-called father had done burned new fury through me, but I'd made it there in time. Thank the gods.

I remained silent, letting her absorb what I was telling her. I was expecting at least another hour of tears, but she suddenly made a growling sound of frustration and threw down the handkerchief. "What is it exactly that you are planning to do with me? Because Gwenda said I was going to live in your villa in the mountains. And I'm *not*."

"You'd rather go back to the innkeeper's care and be sold at his next game of Kings and Bones?"

"Well, I'm not going to go from being his servant to being yours."

"I don't expect you to be my servant." I expected her to be something far more precious.

She stood and paced but couldn't go far in our limited space. Finally, she stopped and crossed her arms on a thick branch, and stared through the leaves at the night sky.

When she spoke, her voice was less accusatory, though frustration radiated from her. "If I was an outcast among the light fae, I'll be a complete pariah among the shadow fae."

The fact the she was even considering living among my people eased the tension tightening my chest. "No one will ever say a word against you, I can promise you that. Also, I live outside the city in a quiet home. My mother lives with me, but she knows about you and is anxious to meet you."

This had her finally turning to look at me, brows lifted in question. "Your mother knows?"

"Of course. She and my father were true mates. They told each other everything."

As true mates should.

She turned back toward the night. "My sister told me that our mother would often leave for a few days at a time when I was young. She'd go to sell herbs and medicine to the next village. But she was often gone much longer than she should be. That was when Papa had kicked her out, thinking she was off sleeping with other men or some nonsense. She wasn't doing that," she snapped vehemently, as if I might argue against her. "At least, I don't think she was unfaithful to Papa after I was born." She shrugged. "I have a knowing about things sometimes."

"No, Murgha. She wasn't."

The finality in my tone must've caught her attention. She turned to face me.

"Do you know what happened to my mother?"

"She went in search of your father. Myrkovir Forest isn't far from Issos. Two days' walk, or one day if she caught a ride by carriage."

"How could you possibly know this?"

"After my father died, I traveled to Issos and discovered your mother had tried to find her mate many times after you were born. He'd disappeared, and she feared the worst."

"For good reason."

I dipped my chin in agreement. "When the innkeeper made her leave, she went to Issos and discovered the truth. She lived there for many years, working for an apothecary."

"She is dead?"

"Yes," I told her honestly. "The apothecary fell ill with the Paviana Plague. Apparently, she nursed him, but contracted it as well. They both died within a year, the locals told me."

She gulped hard, dipping her chin. "I knew she had died. Somehow." She sighed. "The plague," she repeated on a whisper. "None of our clan has been infected, but I hear it is a sad wasting disease, stealing one's magick first."

"That is true. That sickness has not infected any of the

shadow fae either." Though there is another that was far worse taking hold.

"So she died alone." Another tear slid down her cheek. "My poor mother."

"From what the locals told me, she did not suffer. And she was well-respected by all who knew her. She was given good care by the neighbors until the end."

"I don't know how I knew she was dead. But hearing it hurts more."

"I understand. I'm sorry."

She kept quiet for a while, weeping silently. I forced myself to remain rigidly on my side, letting her have a moment to process this news and grieve privately. After a while, she looked at me carefully, her gaze lingering on my wings so long that I cleared my throat to get her attention.

A flush of pink warmed her cheeks, but then she asked boldly, "How did you get into Issos?" She waved a hand at my wings. "There is no way you simply flew into the city and people answered a shadow fae priest's questions."

I smiled. "You're right. They'd never answer a shadow fae. But they would answer a noble Issosian's questions, especially one who dropped a few coins in their pockets."

She scoffed in disbelief, and I was grateful her tears had dried, even if her sadness lingered in the pinched lines around her eyes. "I don't understand."

"Do you know anything about the shadow fae?"

"Only what I've heard. That you're the demons of the sky, enemies to all other fae, killers to all."

I couldn't help but laugh because she was actually serious. "Just because we prefer to live isolated from other fae doesn't make us enemies. And we don't indiscriminately kill others." I sobered. "But we are territorial. We don't like anyone on our mountain."

For their own protection more than anything else.

"None of this explains how you got into Issos without alerting the palace guard and stirring a bee's nest of trouble."

I stood and pulled the rest of the roasted hare from the spit. "Are you still hungry?"

"No, and you're avoiding the question."

I pulled off one last piece and ate it, wondering if I should save it for breakfast. No.

She needed a proper meal in the morning. I threw the remains of the hare out into the night, hearing it break twigs on the way down.

"Vallon."

Her use of my name jarred me. I turned to find her standing only a few feet away. Entranced for a moment by the way the blue light caressed her pretty features, I finally said, "I'm a novgala."

"And what is that?"

"It's probably easier to show you."

"Then show me," she demanded.

For a female who'd been raised to believe she was less than and forced to serve a father who didn't treat her with an ounce of care or love, she was strong-willed and demanding in what she wanted. I liked it. Very much.

She needed to be both of those things if she were to be mine. And she would be.

CHAPTER 8

MURGHA

"ALL RIGHT," VALLON AGREED.

Then he whispered a command in another language. Demon tongue. I'd heard a few wraith fae speak it at the Borderlands when I'd brought my herbs to sell.

He was summoning magick. I could feel it tighten the air around us, a prickling sensation raising gooseflesh on my skin. A whimper escaped my mouth as I hadn't expected the presence of magick like his to feel...pleasurable. It wrapped around me in a cocoon of warmth. Powerful energy sizzled through my body. No wood fae I knew possessed magick as strong as this.

I gasped as Vallon's features disappeared, his form replaced by an Issosian Guard with blond hair, violet eyes, and golden fae wings. I gasped and jumped back.

He grinned, but it wasn't Vallon's striking face that smiled. It was a stranger in the sapphire and gold armor of Issos.

"You can transform yourself," I breathed, taking a tentative step forward to peer closer.

"No. It is illusion only." Vallon's voice came from the Issosian's lips. "I'm not transformed. It is glamour."

I stared in astonishment, shaking my head. "It looks so real." I reached out my hand then drew it back.

"You can touch me. If you like."

Even in the guise of the guard, his gaze was intense and fixed on me. I reached up to the transparent upper wing over his left shoulder where I'd stitched his wound. But before my hand even landed on the fae wing, my fingertips bumped the rough hide of his dragon-like wing. I wrapped my fingers around the edge of bone, which was entirely invisible, like I was clutching onto air.

I laughed as I slid my palm up the invisible line of his wing. "It's remarkable."

He remained silent. But when I glanced up at him, I realized I was standing very close. His breathing was accelerated, but he was still as stone.

I was still holding onto his wing when the illusion melted away to reveal Vallon in all of his magnificence. I might've been terrified when I first saw him enter the inn, and even after when he chased me down and carried me away, but now I couldn't see anything but his masculine beauty—the deep cleft in his chin, the sharp angle of his cheekbones, the softness of his mouth, the radiance of his crimson eyes that looked at me now as if he wanted to devour me.

"A novgala," he said in that low, deep timbre, "uses shadow and light to cast illusion."

"But your illusion looked real, not like simple shadows."

"I am a powerful novgala," he stated with cool confidence. "I can manipulate shadow and light to the most infinitesimal degree."

"Is this why you are high priest of your shadow fae clan?"

"One reason. Someone in my position needs many weapons in his arsenal."

"Why does a priest need weapons? What sort of priest are you exactly?"

He didn't answer, and I still had my hand wrapped around the upper bone of his wing. For some reason, I didn't want to let go. I wanted to hold onto him for forever. It was the strangest sensation, but it was a shockingly strong compulsion. To stay as near to him as I could.

"Is that how you won the game of kings and bones?" I asked, realizing he wasn't going to talk any more about being a priest. Not now anyway.

"Yes. Once we left, my illusion faded, and they could see the rodent skull was sitting on the outer edge of the board, and I hadn't won at all."

"So you won me with a lie."

"I won you with my magick. And if I hadn't, I would've still stolen you away, regardless." His red eyes darkened, his features drawing tight. "I would never have let that ambassador lay a filthy hand on you, Murgha. You are *mine* to protect."

For a breathless second, our gazes held. We were standing so close now I could feel his body heat. "Because of your vow to your father," I clarified softly.

He didn't agree or disagree. He simply stared at me with a feral intensity that had my heart rate tripping faster.

Finally, his gaze trailed up my arm where I was holding onto him. "I believe you should get some rest." His fangs seemed longer, sharper than before. "We have a long day ahead of us tomorrow."

When I finally released him, he closed his eyes and took a step back. "You can sleep there." He pointed to the pile of hides and furs.

"Where will you sleep?"

"I'll keep watch."

While I was aware that my fear of him had vanished into thin air at some point tonight, he was still a large, virile male. Though it wouldn't do me much good if he wanted to harm me, I still wanted protection of some sort.

"I want my dagger," I told him with my palm outstretched.

Instantly, he reached back to his belt and pulled it out and handed it over, hilt first. The dagger was small in his palm, and I suddenly became fascinated by his long, clawed fingertips.

By the goddess, what was happening to me?

I took the dagger and slid it into my scabbard at my belt beneath the coat.

"I have something else," he said softly, opening a pouch on his wide belt. Then he pulled out the thin, gold necklace that was my mother's.

"My *necklace,*" I breathed excitedly.

"Hold up your hair," he commanded. "I'll put it on for you."

I paused for a moment, then turned away from him and lifted my hair out of the way. His large hands came around my front, pulling the strands of the chain on both sides. It seemed remarkable how he was able to be so gentle with the delicate chain and clasp and not break it with his large hands.

One of his claws scraped lightly across my nape as he worked the clasp, sending a shiver down my spine.

"I apologize. Almost done."

The tremble I felt at his nearness, at his claw caressing my skin, had not been one of fear or pain. Quite the opposite.

"There," he said then stepped away.

I peered down at the moonstone I'd cherished so much. I had

no idea he'd snatched it from the pile. I'd thought to never see it again.

"Thank you." I turned to find him seated with his back to the trunk of the wide tree, his wings spread, his booted feet crossed at the ankles. "This necklace is important to me," I admitted.

"I know." His eyes glittered by the blue coal-fire.

Without another word, I lay down on the makeshift bed, pulling one of the hides over me, facing away from him toward the fire and Gwenda, who was still sleeping soundly.

My mind rewound to the story of my mother. And my real father. The pain of their tragic tale sank deep. I blinked back the tears and closed my eyes, trying to imagine what it would've been like for my mother to find her true mate after she was already married.

The gods had a fate designed for everyone, if one believed in the gods. And I did.

I devoted myself to Elska, Goddess of the Wood. Though we had no temple in our new village since we'd left Myrkovir Forest, I still paid tribute to her with floral coronets of juniper and night phlox, believed to be her favorite flowers. I set them around the largest oak tree in the woods behind the house, creating my own temple for her. I prayed to her weekly, hoping for her blessings.

I'd once prayed for Mama to return, but then realized Tessa was all the family I needed. Then one night, Tessa went out to find medicine for father and never returned, so perhaps the goddess didn't care for me much.

Maybe I was to have a tragic end like my mother, destined to never find the correct path until it was too late. Never to have a mate as the half-breed pariah that I was.

"Your father loved your mother," came the velvet dark voice of the shadow fae. "And he loved you. Of that, you can be certain.

The only reason he didn't take her away to Issos was because she told him she couldn't abandon your sister."

I believed him. But it didn't ease the sad ache blooming in my heart. It only made it spread wider, making me feel more alone than ever before.

CHAPTER 9

MURGHA

I awoke from a restless sleep to a light tinkling sound and the soft chirp of morning larks. As the fuzz of a dream I couldn't remember peeled away, memories of yesterday and last night returned to me. I bolted upright. What I saw immediately pulled a smile to my lips.

Vallon sat cross-legged on the far side of the coal-fire still burning, for I could feel its heat and see the dim glow in the gray morning light. He was hunched over, murmuring softly to Gwendazelle, who was crouched on the branch she'd slept upon, both of them holding ornate, silver teacups.

I rubbed my eyes and uncurled from the nest of blankets, my tummy rumbling at the sweet, spicy scent. They both looked up.

"Good morning," said Vallon casually, taking a sip of tea.

"Morning, Murgha," chirped Gwenda, sipping from her own

tiny cup that seemed to be an exact replica of Vallon's, only much, much smaller.

I blinked sleepily, wondering if I was dreaming. Between them was a steaming silver pot and a matching creamer decanter upon a small, silver tray.

Yesterday, when this terrifying shadow fae stormed into Papa's inn and swept me away by force, I never imagined this picture of him sitting daintily with a pretty wood sprite, sipping morning tea from an obviously expensive and ornamental tea set.

"Do you like tea?" he asked.

"I love tea," I told him honestly. Though I had never drunk from a service such as this.

"Have a seat." He gestured toward the hide that was still spread out on his side of the fire, where I'd sat and interrogated him last night.

I sat, cross-legged, facing the tea set, admiring it as he poured a steaming cup.

"Do you take cream?"

I nodded. "I smell cinnamon. What is that other sweet smell?"

"Dried maragord peels and rose hips. It's a simple tea, but one I prefer."

I wanted to cry from sheer joy. Maragord was a delectable fruit that I rarely got the chance to eat. It grew in Northgall and the northern parts of Lumeria. It was utterly delicious.

I watched him pour the cream, his broad, clawed hands and long fingers looking elegant as he carefully served me tea. When I took the cup and sipped, he watched me carefully. I hummed with pleasure and smiled at the spicy sweetness and the richness of the cream. It tasted better than any tea I'd ever made for myself.

"This is delicious," I admitted warmly.

He smiled. "Good."

We sat in companionable silence, the three of us sipping tea as the world came awake with more chirping of birds in the forest. I admired the silver cup in my hand, an ornate, engraved design that looked like dragon wings but were actually those of a shadow fae with swirling flourishes that repeated all the way around.

I pointed at Gwenda. "You had a cup made for her?"

"Gwenda loves tea," was his simple answer.

He didn't explain how he apparently cared a great deal for the wood sprite. Gwenda smiled, flashing her serrated teeth before sipping again, the tiny teacup in both of her hands.

"They make these in Gadlizel?"

"You sound surprised."

"I suppose I am."

"Gadlizel is an extremely civilized city. We enjoy our tea as much as the next fae."

I laughed. "I enjoy my tea in an earthenware cup with a chip on one side. This is far fancier than I'm used to."

"You should have all the luxuries your heart desires." His voice rumbled with silky sincerity.

For a moment, I was caught at the truth of it. He believed I deserved better. Besides Tessa, he was the first person to ever wish something more for me. I had to change the subject.

"What does Gadlizel look like?"

He finished his cup and set it on the tray. "It is a vast city spread across a valley midway up the Solgavia Mountains. The palace is closer to the peak. Our buildings are made of a pale slate that we quarry nearby. We have fine craftsman and artisans that have made the city one of the most beautiful in all the realms."

"Is it more beautiful than Silvantis or Issos?" Those were the two great cities of Northgall and Lumeria.

"Much more beautiful." He watched me, his gaze dipping to my mouth when I sipped my tea.

"I'd like to see Gadlizel."

A crease formed between his brow before he set his cup on the tray. "You will. But we will stay in my villa for a time. It's above the city proper."

I didn't want to wreck the peaceful morning, but I couldn't refrain from telling him, "I want to search for my sister."

He didn't appear surprised.

"If she's alive and truly living with the beast fae," I continued, "then I must find her."

"I know," he said calmly. "I knew you would want to. But first, I must report to my prince. I've been away from Gadlizel for too long."

"You've been here?" I gestured around us. "For how long?"

His gaze remained steady and poised. "A few months."

He'd been camped up here in this makeshift shelter for months? Watching out for me?

"Why couldn't you keep an eye on me from afar like your father did?"

He clamped his jaw tight and stood. "We should get moving."

I finished my tea in one last gulp then handed him the cup. While he set about emptying the portable pit of blue-coal and packing it away, I found my brush at the bottom of my bag.

Gwenda perched on a branch and watched me with a contented smile as I untangled and unwound the small braids at my temples.

"It must look like a mess."

She shook her head. "So pretty."

I brushed through my mass of hair several times, very aware of Vallon moving around, stealing glances at me while he packed.

By the time he was done, I'd managed to braid my hair into

one long rope. I thought it more practical for travel, to keep it out of my way. Once I'd stored my brush in my bag, I turned to find him waiting with his own rucksack slung over one shoulder.

"Ready?" he asked.

I was, of course, but then I realized I was about to be in his arms, flying high above the ground. When my pulse rocketed, I wasn't sure if it was at the thought of flying again or being pressed so close to his body.

I nodded, and he closed the space between us, staring down at me with that enigmatic, cool expression. His crimson gaze was so intense I had to bite my lip to keep a whimper of pleasure from escaping. His nearness made me dizzy with an unquestionable desire. Heat crawled up my chest and neck, flushing my cheeks.

His gaze wandered over my face. "Don't be nervous," he said in that deep timbre of his.

"I'm not."

When a sudden wind rustled the leaves, a strand of my hair I'd missed crossed my face and caught on my lip. He lifted his hand, and I didn't move as he slowly removed the lock with one finger and tucked it behind my ear. His claw gently scraped my scalp, the pad of his finger gliding along the shell of my ear.

He watched me with careful scrutiny. Then he scooped me into his arms. I sucked in a breath and quickly wrapped my arms around his neck.

"Comfortable?" he asked.

As comfortable as I could be in a shadow fae's arms. I wanted to laugh, but I simply nodded.

He looked up, revealing the line of his thick, masculine throat. I was shocked at my sudden desire to bury my face there and inhale deeply of his scent.

Some madness must have come over me. I didn't even know

this male, and my entire being—heart, soul, and body—was wholly entranced by him.

So what if he'd saved me from being gambled away to that disgusting ambassador? I would've run away from Rukard if he'd won me in the game. And sure, Vallon had also had enough care to grab my necklace for me. He had honor in heeding his father's dying wish. But I'd admired many similar males before and not had this visceral, aroused reaction to them.

He was a foreigner. A dark fae. By all accounts, an enemy to our kind.

Then why did he feel like the opposite to me, like a trusted friend I've been waiting for all my life?

He flew north, the sun slowly rising to the east and glazing the world in gold. Yet again, I became fascinated by the way the landscape looked from up here.

"Are you warmer in the new clothes?" His chest rumbled, his voice close and intimate even while the wind rushed over us.

"Yes." I hadn't realized how drafty and uncomfortable my dress had been from this height until he asked. "Thank you for the clothes."

"You're welcome."

Down below, I could see a cluster of small buildings spread out in a curving line. "That's the Borderlands?"

The Borderlands weren't a village of any particular kind. And it was home to many different kinds of fae—light and dark. It was literally a string of sporadic inns, houses, and shops selling wares to anyone who passed between Lumeria and Northgall.

"Yes," he answered.

"Is that where we're going?"

He began to descend, flapping his wings once then soaring on air.

"I need to get a decent meal into you before our longer trek into the mountains."

He didn't land next to what looked to be a tavern and inn as I'd expected. Instead, he slowed and dropped behind a copse of trees close to the inn. From here, I could read the sign hanging over the door with bright yellow lettering—The Black Boar.

He set me on my feet, his large hand steadying me before he let go.

"Are we hiding from someone?" I asked as he peered through the thin grove of trees at the inn.

"Merely being cautious. Making sure no other Mevian guards are looking for you."

I'd been so consumed with my captor at the time, I hadn't thought about those guards. Strange how a mere few hours could change everything. I had no intention of escaping now or ever going back.

"What happened to the other guards in my village?"

"One is dead. The other had better found a healer by now if he wanted to save his arm." Then he walked on casually ahead of me.

I hurried to catch up. "Dead?"

A frown creased his brow. "They tried to kill me if you recall. I thought I was being kind to let one live."

An uncomfortable laugh bubbled up my throat. "Very kind."

"Would you have preferred they kill me? Then drag you off to be that abhorrent lecher's property?"

He was offended, and I realized quickly I didn't want to hurt him, not even in the smallest way. I'm not sure where these protective instincts came from in regard to Vallon, but I couldn't do anything besides act on them.

"Of course not." I shrugged. "It's just that sword fights to the death aren't something I normally witness. Actually, I've never seen a physical altercation like that in my life." Though I had run away before I had seen much of it at all. But I had seen Vallon deftly dodge and swing his sword, fighting two at once with practiced ease.

"I've lived a rather quiet, sheltered life away from violence and war," I added.

"You're fortunate in that regard."

I huffed a small laugh. "I suppose I'm a little shocked that anyone was fighting over me in the first place. That's never happened, even if it likely had more to do with the guardsmen's pride than anything else."

Vallon pulled me to a stop and faced me, his large hand wrapped around my forearm. His expression had hardened into sharp, tight angles. "The fact that no male saw fit that you were and are a female worth fighting for is their loss. But I'm here now." He shifted closer, those crimson eyes bewitching in their intensity. "And I'll kill anyone who dares to even touch you."

For a breathless moment, I simply stared back, soaking in his lethal promise. I tried for levity, smiling as I said, "You've taken your father's vow very seriously."

His answering reply was a sweeping examination of my face, ending at my mouth. Then he dropped my arm and urged me forward with a hand at my back. "Let's get you something to eat."

CHAPTER 10

MURGHA

After Tessa disappeared and Papa had recovered from his illness, I'd begged him to gather some fae males and look for her. Other than search near the stream where she'd gone that night, he'd done nothing at all.

Well, that's not entirely true. Because Tessa was his favorite child, of course, he sank into a depression for a time, drinking and gambling even more than before she'd gone.

Though I'd always believed her letter was coerced, I wondered now if it were true. She'd given me an option to join her with her beast fae mate and his clan, but the idea had seemed so ludicrous at the time. I'd laughed at the very idea of leaving the safety of my home.

But my home wasn't safe. I could see in the bitterness of Papa's stares and his lack of any care at all for me that I was in danger.

So I'd gathered some herbs to sell and ventured to the Border-lands a few times, seeking any word or news of my sister. I was terrified at first, seeing wraith fae for the first time. I'd even seen two beast fae females traveling with a child.

No one had heard of my sister or of a beast fae male abducting a wood fae. To my surprise, the dark fae I'd met on my few trips were kind and courteous, if a little wary.

So I wasn't nervous about entering The Black Boar, even in the company of a shadow fae who were rarely, if ever, seen in these parts. He was the first of his kind I'd ever encountered. I wondered if they were all as magnificent as him.

He ushered me inside and to a booth in the corner, facing the window. In the rest of the tavern, there was only a wraith fae couple—both two-horned and dressed in well-made, homespun clothes. The male watched us with a curious expression but returned to his meal when Vallon pointedly glared at him.

After we settled into opposite seats, the table between us, I gave him an exasperated look.

"What?" he snapped.

"You don't have to stare at him so angrily. He has done nothing to you."

"That's correct. And now he knows to stay out of my way."

"Why would he bother you at all?"

He exhaled heavily and leaned forward, speaking low. "Because my kind aren't liked by the other dark fae, much less any Lumerians we come across."

"Why don't they like you?"

"Because we keep to ourselves and defend our mountains at all costs. It's created several altercations in the past. And a war or two."

"Oh, just a war or two, that's not so bad."

His glacial expression didn't crack at my teasing sarcasm.

"Why are you protecting the mountains?" I asked him.

"We've always protected the mountains." His voice had dropped deeper.

"That's not an answer," I snapped back.

Our gazes held. His jaw was clamped tight as he refused to tell me what he was hiding.

Finally, I broke the tension-laced silence. "If you're so concerned about being attacked, why not change your appearance? Maybe back to that handsome Issosian guard you mimicked last night?"

His expression hardened further, and when he leaned across the table, his clawed fingers clasped in a forced relaxed posture, his voice had darkened to a dangerous level. "You found him handsome, did you?"

"Of course, I did."

But not nearly as handsome as you.

"Is that what you're attracted to?" He sneered. "Soft-faced golden boys?"

I blinked at him, speechless, for I was positively sure his anger was jealousy.

I'd always been the biddable, good daughter. Always trying to make up for the deficiencies of my birth, hoping that if I were good enough, Papa might finally love me. That someone might love me beyond Tessa.

But something had changed yesterday. When Papa had gambled me away like I was nothing more than a piece of property he was readily willing to lose, a crack opened up inside of me. Rather than fall into the deep abyss, it opened wide a new door, a new world. One where I didn't need to be the good daughter anymore.

Then this stranger had appeared and whisked me away from all that I knew, changed me into strange clothes, and in telling me the truth, gave me back not only my mother, but my father. They had loved each other, and they had loved me.

The Murgha sitting across from the fuming shadow fae was not the meek girl I had been before. A tendril of heat and excitement threaded through my belly at the angry dark fae staring at me as if he truly wanted to eat me alive.

I should be shaking with fear, but the shiver that skated down my spine had nothing at all to do with fear. It was thick, sweet desire. And I wanted more of it. So I did the only thing I could do. I teased him.

"The Issosian you transformed into was undeniably attractive. Do you know him? Is he someone you might introduce me to?"

"He is no one. Someone I met in my travels. And you will *never* meet him."

"Why not?"

"Because I don't like—"

He didn't finish the sentence. I arched a brow, waiting for more, but then a waitress appeared at our table.

"Morning. Aren't you two an interesting pair?"

Vallon's hard gaze shot to her, but she merely raised one hand, palm out. Her splayed hand revealed the webbing of skin between her fingers. She was a skald fae.

"I meant no offense, priest. What can I get for you two this morning?"

"What do you have?" he grumbled.

"We've got wild hog ham, fresh bread, an assortment of cheese, poached eggs, spiced berry jam, and honey-and-cream oats."

"Bring us two servings of everything. And a pot of tea." Then Vallon looked past her toward the bar. "Is Haldek in the back?"

"He is."

Vallon leaned over the table, catching my gaze with that intensity that was becoming far too familiar. "I'll be right back. Stay here." Then he shoved out of the booth and strode toward a door next to the bar that must lead to the kitchen area.

When I turned my attention back to the skald fae, I found her observing me carefully. I couldn't help but admire her striking features.

Her hair was a vibrant red, like that of a cloak I had seen and coveted once on a Mevian fae who'd passed through our village. Her eyes were jewel green, the color I imagined the Nemian Sea might be. The skald fae lived in Morodon next to the sea named after their sea god.

"You're far from home," she said to me finally.

"So are you," I observed.

When she smiled, her wide mouth and feline-shaped eyes only made her look more striking. I'd always thought myself fair, but she was as pale as parchment.

There was something else about her that tingled my senses, making gooseflesh rise on my arms. That always happened when my seer abilities sprang to the forefront. But I didn't have a vision or a flash of knowing, just a hint of something I couldn't quite put my finger on.

She glanced over her shoulder before she leaned closer. "Do you need help?"

I almost laughed. Yesterday afternoon, I would've begged anyone for help to get away from the giant shadow fae who'd abducted me. But today, he was no longer my enemy. He was my ally. And he was going to help me find my sister.

"No," I said with a smile.

Then she arched her brow with a wicked expression. "Ah, I see now." She winked. "Let me just get that breakfast for you then."

She swished off in her plain, brown dress that only accentuated her vibrant coloring all the more and went through the door where Vallon had disappeared. I was surprised she jumped to the conclusion that Vallon and I were—what—lovers? More than that?

The idea flipped my belly with nerves. For so many reasons. Strangely, none of them were because I abhorred the idea.

The wraith fae couple ate their breakfast and murmured softly, not even looking my way. The tavern was built with better craftsmanship than my Papa's. Not my Papa, I suppose. Not anymore. I had to keep reminding myself.

There were sturdy beams across the ceiling, carved from the pale gray trunks of esher trees. That would've cost the owner a pretty penny seeing as eshers only grew far to the north near Silvantis.

The tables and chairs were crafted with flourishing designs that showed the artisan had an artist's eye, not simply the practical eye of a builder. The tall and wide fireplace was built of large, smooth river stones someone had to have hauled with great care or purchased at a hefty price.

The skald fae entered through the swinging kitchen door and returned to my booth with a pot of tea that smelled of spiced cloves and redberries, a lovely combination, though not as sweet and tempting as Vallon's.

She set two ceramic cups on the table and a decanter of cream. I bit back a smile, remembering Vallon's fancy, silver tea service high in the tree this morning.

"Thank you," I told her.

"You're welcome." She propped a hand on her hip. "Where are you two headed?"

"The Solgavia Mountains," I told her easily, not knowing any reason I shouldn't, my gaze straying to her webbed hand on her hip. "Why are you living so far from Morodon?"

"Why are you living so far from the forests of Lumeria?" She quirked a dark red brow at me, a deeper shade than her hair.

I laughed. "Many reasons."

"I see. Same for me."

"I'm Murgha," I told her, reaching out a hand.

She shook it. "Jessamine."

The outer door opened. Jessamine stiffened but then relaxed when she saw the two wraith fae step into the tavern. Actually, when the tiny female removed her cloak, I could see small black wings tucked against her back. Like Vallon's. She had the dark gray complexion of a wraith fae and two delicate horns curling back over her fine black hair that was cut short.

The wraith fae male she was with was big and brawny, wearing black armor and silver bands on his four horns, designating him of some importance. One of his horns was broken.

"Back so soon," Jessamine called to them.

The one with the broken horn looked her way, smiling brightly, revealing he was missing an eye. Despite his scarred face, he appeared a gentle soul. That knowledge hummed in my breast, making me feel at ease.

"Just passing through, Jessamine. Heading back to Silvantis."

Jessamine turned to me. "Be right back with your breakfast." Then she walked over to the newcomers who had settled in a booth on the wall opposite from me.

"Tea or ale?"

"Ale for me," said the broken-horned fae. "Tea for Hava."

Vallon stepped back through the door, his gaze shooting to me first and then the new wraith fae. Rather than dart them murderous looks as I'd expected, his expression relaxed, a small smile quirking his lips.

Jessamine marched away, passing Vallon on her way back into

the kitchen. Rather than rejoin me, Vallon walked over to the two newcomers.

"Well, well. Didn't expect to see you in this neck of the woods, priest," said the broken-horned one.

They knew each other then.

"Keffa." Vallon nodded at him. "You either. On an errand for the king?"

"Just left him at Windolek Castle."

Vallon grunted. "I heard the queen is healthy and thriving after giving birth to his heir."

This was new news to me, but I smiled at the memory of having met Princess Una once, now the Queen of Northgall and Lumeria. It felt like a lifetime ago that she'd passed through our village in Myrkovir Forest during the Autumnal Solstice celebration, when I had scried my first true vision. I'd never told Tessa because I couldn't quite believe it myself. I'd been given one of the greatest gifts from the gods—the ability to see prophecy.

When I'd tried to tell Tessa that I believed my magick, which hadn't shown up before then, might be that of a seer, she had told me it was impossible. Wood fae didn't have that kind of magick. And though she knew as well as I that I wasn't a full-blooded wood fae, it seemed to dishearten her that I might be so different from her.

So I stopped talking about it. Perhaps my feelings were nothing more than paranoia. Or basic intuition.

It didn't matter. I never had to tell Tessa again because I had never had any other visions after that single time I'd given one to Princess Una. But I could feel the magick stirring again, that same deep well of energy, an overflow of force. Like it was waiting for something.

"She is doing well," the female with the broken-horned fae said excitedly. "As is their babe. All are fine and healthy."

"I don't believe you met my mate before," the one named Keffa said. "This is Hava."

"We weren't mates then," the female said teasingly to Keffa.

Vallon dipped his chin. "Greetings, Hava." He turned back to Keffa. "I'm surprised you didn't stay with King Gollaya."

"He needs me in Näkt Mir. Tending to business while he's away."

"Must be good to be the king."

"It is now," agreed Keffa, his voice more somber. A heaviness seemed to pause their conversation, and then Keffa asked, "What are you doing in the Borderlands, priest?"

"Tending to some business of my own."

"Your business involve that pretty, fair-haired light fae over there?"

I looked away, sipping my tea, when I felt both their gazes on me. I hadn't realized the wraith fae named Keffa had even noticed me.

Jessamine returned carrying a heavy tray of dishes. "Here you are, Murgha," she said, piling them on the table.

My stomach growled at the small feast, especially when I saw the bowl of fresh-whipped butter.

"Thank you." I dove into the breadbasket first.

"Enjoy."

As she sauntered off, Vallon took his seat again.

"How do you know those wraith fae?" I asked.

"Some business with the king and his mizrah last year. They needed our help with...something."

Glancing over, I couldn't help but stare at the unusual female with wings. Wraith fae didn't have wings.

"Yes," said Vallon, seeming to peer into my thoughts, "she's half wraith and shadow fae."

"That's unusual, isn't it?" I didn't know that different dark fae mated.

"It is. But not unheard of."

I grew silent a moment, ruminating on myself as a half-breed light fae. For once, I didn't feel the shame that always accompanied such thoughts.

"I met her once," I said, putting some white cheese onto my plate. "Princess Una."

"When was this?" he asked curiously, forking some ham onto his plate.

"Years ago. Before we left Myrkovir. She was very kind."

And the gods spoke to me for the first time that day. They'd wanted me to tell my vision to the princess. So I had.

"You and the skald fae seem friendly." He changed the subject, obviously not wanting to discuss her or the king or how and why they'd met before.

"She's a friendly person. Is there a reason I shouldn't be?"

"Not especially." He poured himself some tea. "She's just a curious one."

"You've met her before?"

"Yes. Though she doesn't know it. I usually come here shadowed as someone else. But the owner, Haldek, knows the real me. We've helped each other with information before."

"What about Jessamine? What's curious about her?"

"She's a skald fae far from home and far from water. Skald fae need water to keep their magick strong. I can sense magick in her, though I have no idea what her gift from the gods might be."

Like all fae, the skald people held gifts that were more aligned to their natural abilities. Some were willodens, water-wielders. Some could speak to and befriend naiads. Naiads were notoriously fierce and cruel, hating most of fae kind, so to be able to connect with one was a god-given gift. Some skald fae could even speak to the fish and mammals of the sea.

"You're right." I frowned, watching Jessamine deliver ale and tea to the newcomers with a bright smile. "I can sense her magick as well. It should be dimmed being so far away from the sea."

"She's hiding something," said Vallon.

"Maybe she's hiding from someone." I set my piece of bread on my plate, wiping my mouth with my napkin and wondering if Papa or Rukard would send more after me.

My pulse leaped with fear of being dragged back to the village. I wanted to laugh at the turn of events in less than a full day.

Vallon wore that intense expression again, his hard gaze on me. "If the man who raised you or the Mevian sends anyone after you, I'll kill them, Murgha."

"You don't have to murder anyone," I whispered. "A sound beating will do."

"It wouldn't be murder. It would be justice."

"Nevertheless, we don't have to leave a trail of bodies behind us. That might make us easier to find."

"I'd love for them to find us." He forked a piece of ham into his mouth. "Need to do something with this...aggression."

"Why *are* you so aggressive? Since we left our little treehouse, you've been so moody, like you're ready to flay people alive."

I spooned some honey onto the bread and ate a huge bite, licking the spot of honey off my lip. Vallon's attention was solely on my mouth. I stopped chewing, suddenly self-conscious. But his focus didn't waver, the red of his irises slowly being absorbed by the black.

I swallowed the bread, the bite going down thickly. His gaze skimmed down my throat, which only increased my pulse, pounding hard at the base.

Vallon eased his back against the booth, flattening his wings wide, and finally met my gaze again. "I'll let you know what the aggression is about soon enough, but I'm beginning to think you know."

"I don't." Though perhaps I had *some* idea.

"I'll show you when we get to my home in the Solgavia Mountains." His look was savage, predatory.

"What if I don't want you to show me?"

That was what finally cracked his expression. But his smile with a hint of fang was not disarming at all. It only catapulted my pulse faster.

"It's too late for that, Murgha."

CHAPTER 11

VALLON

Leaving Haldek's place and being back in the sky with her safely in my arms should've calmed me. It didn't. If anything, it only amplified the heart-rattling emotions beginning to consume my every thought.

She'd been quiet since we left, her expression serious. We'd been flying for a few hours. Other than me pointing out landmarks I thought she might be interested in like when we crossed over Lake Moreen, I'd also remained silent.

"Aren't you getting tired?" she asked, the wind having pulled strands of her hair loose.

Every now and then, the wind would blow a silken strand against my neck or chin, the soft caresses torturous.

"It might be good to rest a few minutes." It would be good for me to take a break from her intoxicating scent and the soft warmth of her body in my arms. "Besides, you look cold."

Her cheeks were pink from the constant beat of the wind, and it was beginning to concern me. She wasn't shivering, but the temperatures had dropped dramatically since we'd been flying directly north for several hours. Summer in the mountains felt like winter in Lumeria where she was from.

"A warm fire would be good for a bit," she agreed.

We were directly over the higher foothills of the Solgavia Mountains. I beat my wings and banked us down toward a winding stream. We could fill our canteens there as well.

When we landed, I set her on her feet, then took a moment to wind my arms backward to rotate my shoulder muscles that had become tight and stiff from holding her so long.

"Sorry about that," she said, watching me.

"I'm fine," I assured her.

"Where's Gwenda?"

"She likes to go off by herself, but she always finds me."

Murgha nodded while looking around at the gurgling brook flowing with the clear blue water of snow-melt from high in the Solgavias. There was sparse vegetation, but a lone, thick-trunked elm tree sprouted in a nice spot with some flat stones.

I observed the entire area, seeking any signs of danger. I hadn't seen anyone, but I sensed there may be shadow fae nearby. There should be a patrol on guard a little higher up. The fact that I hadn't seen anyone should've eased my tension, but it didn't.

Prince Torvyn had grown more distant over the past year. Who could blame him with the king's maddening rages? But even that wasn't what set all of us on edge, what had caused our corps of priests to become more and more vigilant. The evil was spreading, and our efforts to suppress it were futile.

Murgha stepped along the brook, smiling serenely. She wanted to know why we guarded the mountain. I'd have to tell her eventually. But for now, I wanted to keep that ugly truth to myself.

My gaze caught on something farther up the stream. Instantly, I walked toward it, passing Murgha, but as I did, I took her hand gently in mine.

She startled but didn't pull away.

"Come see," I said, tugging her toward the bush.

She followed, letting me hold her small hand in mine. That simple touch accelerated my heart rate. Yet again, that deep ache in my fangs, the need to put my mark on her, was growing fierce.

A shadow fae didn't hesitate when he found his mate. He simply took her. It was common among my kind. Our females understood. Often, they'd fight the male off. He'd have to prove himself worthy of claiming her by dominating her in battle, then in bed. If he could subdue her, then he was good enough for her to accept his bite.

But Murgha wasn't a shadow fae female, born with the gifts of a warrior and of illusion. She couldn't get away from me if she tried. So small. So delicate. A hard possessiveness clutched me in an iron fist.

So I wouldn't heed the desperate urge burning a hole inside my chest, pushing me to grip her hard, hold her down, and sink my teeth and cock inside her. Not yet.

"Look." My voice was deep and rough, but I kept a gentle hold on her hand, showing her what I'd seen.

She gasped. "Dellabore!"

Letting my hand go, she rushed forward and kneeled before the flowering bush. The black-pedaled leaves gleamed with a silky sheen even on this cloudy day.

"They're so beautiful," she marveled, beaming up at me.

Her smile made her more lovely, the sight tearing into me a little deeper.

"I'll go make a fire."

"Can I take some of the flower petals? Will they harm me?"

"There's no toxin in the petals or the leaves but use your dagger. They're tough. And be careful of the spikes on the leaves."

She was pulling her dagger from the scabbard as I turned and headed back down the small incline. I needed more space. I needed a moment to quell this growing desire I couldn't seem to control.

Shaking my head at myself, I pulled the portable firepit from my satchel. I'd always been a man of control, the High Priest of Gadlizel with unshakable nerve and poise. Torvyn would laugh if he saw me now, completely undone by a tiny, fair-haired light fae.

I'd told the prince—and my best friend—where I'd been going the past many months. He knew of my vow to my father, but he also knew my duty to him and to Gadlizel came first. At least, it had...before I'd seen her. Before I'd realized she was my divine mate, given to me by the gods.

I'd always imagined my mate would be a fierce warrior, perhaps touched with golden hair by Solzkin himself. I imagined she might be serious and strong with great black wings, so the two of us could soar high over the peaks together.

I could never in my wildest fantasies have imagined that she would be someone like Murgha—small and sweet and so very vulnerable. My heart twisted.

She had no wings to escape danger, no training as a warrior. Though she could wield a tiny dagger fast enough. I smiled at the memory of her holding it to my throat, ready to defend herself. Her courage was greater than any shadow fae female I'd ever known. Murgha had every reason to cower against an opponent twice her size, but she didn't.

After setting up the blue coal fire, I went about pulling out the bread and cheese that Jessamine had wrapped for us. Murgha might be hungry.

Standing, I peered up the stream, not seeing her at the dellabore bush. "Murgha?"

Instantly, I climbed back up to the rocky slope where I'd left her. Right as I reached the dellabore bush, a gasping scream echoed from around a boulder.

"Murgha!"

In a flash, I was around the corner, my gaze falling to her dagger sitting on the edge of a crevasse in the mountainside. Instantly, I was on my belly, peering inside the narrow opening.

"Murgha!" I sensed and smelled her in the darkness.

"I'm here," her voice echoed shakily.

"Are you hurt?"

"I fell on something sharp. My arm is scraped a little." Her voice trembled, and her pulse quickened. "Vallon?"

"Hang on. I think I can loosen these stones here and squeeze down to you." She'd fallen through a crack where the stone had crumbled and come loose, but there was another scent wafting from down below that I didn't like.

"Vallon?"

On my knees, I pulled loose a stone as wide as my chest and dropped it aside. "I'm coming."

Her voice trembled more as she said in a near whisper, "I think there's something down here with me."

Falling back onto my belly, I peered through the wider opening, my gut twisting with blood-chilling fear.

"Don't move," I warned in a low voice. "Be very still."

Murgha tilted her pale face up at the opening, squinting in the dark at the light above and holding her bleeding arm. Surrounding her in a mountainous spill into the shadows were piles and piles of bones.

CHAPTER 12

MURGHA

I FROZE, MORE FROM THE DEADLY TONE OF HIS VOICE THAN HIS command. He removed another stone, more gray light spilling through the crevice above into the pit where I'd fallen. That's when I saw what I was sitting upon.

Scattered and broken, some still with flesh clinging to them, I had fallen into a den of bones. A predator's den. They weren't the remnants of deer or boar or other large prey. They were the skulls, legs, arms, and wings of dead fae. One of the skulls, completely white with two giant spiraling horns, was that of a beast fae. The jaw was open in a soundless scream.

But not even that was what had my heart pumping hard with fear. There was something foul filling this space, a dark essence that awakened my magick with a burning sensation blazing through my veins. It hurt. I whimpered.

"I can't breathe," I whispered to myself, my chest rising and falling so quickly I began to feel dizzy.

"I'm coming!" Vallon shouted from overhead, removing another stone from the opening.

Then a low, sinister rumble filled the cavern. In the deep shadows, four eyes glowed silver in the dark.

"Murgha, listen to me." Vallon's voice was deep and urgent. "Do not move. It will not be able to see you if you *don't* move. He can smell you, but my shield will confuse his senses."

I didn't ask what he meant. In the next second, I was encased in a gray shroud, magick covering me like a blanket. Instinctively, I knew that it was Vallon's magick. He'd swathed me in shadow, so the bones around me became a smudged blur. And though I could barely see those four eyes growing closer, it was the feel of this beast that had me trembling with terror.

The clamor of stones being shifted and Vallon's labored breathing above felt distant as I homed in on the creature crawling closer to me. When it slithered near the light, to keep from making a sound, I bit on my bottom lip so hard I tasted blood.

It slid across the cavern floor and over piles of bones with a giant serpentine body, its horned head nearly scraping the top of the cavern. But it wasn't a serpent entirely. It had eight muscular legs that ended in long black claws as long as my arm. The creature's forked tongue lanced the air and then it hissed, revealing rows and rows of long, sharp fangs.

Vallon was right. His shadow magick had kept me completely camouflaged. Barely even breathing, I remained perfectly still as it slithered over a mound of bones, sending several skulls rolling to the side.

My heart pounded so hard I thought it would leap from my chest as it came even closer, bringing with it a wave of evil so potent I sucked in a breath. This creature wasn't simply a preda-tor. It was filled with something malevolent and wicked.

It moved farther into the light, heading toward me slowly, it's black, forked tongue licking the air. Its scales were a pattern of shiny silver and dark gray would make it blend into the mountain when hunting prey. But right now, it didn't need to hide. It simply needed to find me. If it stepped five steps to the right, its forked tongue would lick right across my face.

I pulled my injured arm closer to my chest, dislodging a femur bone at my elbow that went rolling down the small hill. The crea-ture jerked its giant head in my direction and opened its jaws with a terrifying hiss. It knew where I was. It coiled its body upward ready to strike.

Blessed Mother of the Wood, protect me.

Then the beating of huge, black wings dragged my attention upward. Vallon dove through the opening like a falling star, his sword poised above him in both hands. The beast was so intent on me that it looked up too late.

Vallon landed on its head and sank its sword into its eye up to the hilt. The creature screamed so loud I covered my ears. It shook back and forth, trying to dislodge Vallon, but my shadow fae was stabbing over and over, gouging out one eye then moving to the other.

When I thought the monster had kicked him off balance he'd actually leaped to the floor of bones, dragging his sword across the creature's throat. It hissed and screamed, black blood spewing as it scrambled backward to flee into its den. But Vallon had already given the death blow. Before the serpent completely withdrew into the shadows, it collapsed onto its pile of bones, black tongue hanging from its mouth.

Suddenly, the gray haze was gone and Vallon had me in his arms. Then we were airborne, and he flew us back through the crevice above. His wings scraped the edges as we passed through the opening and shot straight up then down the small incline to where the blue coal-fire was burning. There was unwrapped cheese and bread scattered on the ground.

He set me on a large stone next to the stream, the soft babbling water a sharp contrast to the suffocating silence of that den.

Chest heaving, Vallon bent over the stream and splashed the water on his hands and arms where the blood of the creature had splattered. I watched him stalk back to his satchel, yank out a cloth, and frantically wipe the creature's remnants off him, swiping the towel across his face as well.

"Your wings," I murmured as I gulped in the fresh air, no longer stifled by the oppressive stench of death and evil down below.

"My wings?" he huffed with exasperation, his voice trembling as he finally turned to me.

Tossing the cloth onto the rocks near the coal-fire, he strode toward me, his expression tight and stern. He gripped me by the shoulders and hauled me roughly to my feet. Then, very gently, he cupped my face, his hands shaking. I instinctively covered his hands with mine, needing to comfort him. So strange it was what had been running through my mind—that Vallon needed me to soothe him, and it was my place to do so.

"You hurt your wings on the rocks," I whispered dumbly as he held me so intimately.

"Fuck my wings, Murgha." He pressed his forehead to mine. "I almost lost *you*."

"You didn't," I whispered, tilting my face closer to his.

Then we were sharing breaths, and that deep, aching longing for the affection of another hit me with ferocity. He didn't bridge the tiny space between our mouths, so I dared to do it myself.

Lightly, I brushed my lips across his. "I'm here."

He stiffened for a moment, then ever-so-gently he grazed his mouth against mine. The sensation was divine. Pure loveliness.

He coaxed and teased my lips apart then sank into my mouth on a groan. When his tongue touched mine, I kissed him back with desperate need. I stroked mine against his, slowly sliding my tongue along one of his fangs.

One of his arms came around my waist, lifting me against his hard body. I felt his stiffened cock against my belly, and my reaction wasn't at all what I would've thought. It shocked me that I wanted to open my legs and take him inside me.

I had the uncontrollable urge to touch him, to feel him. I glided my hands up his broad shoulders and clasped them beneath his hair at his nape.

He moaned into my mouth, pressing me closer. With one hand, he encircled the back of my neck, his thumb resting on the pulse at the base of my throat. His other hand slid down my spine to my backside, cupping me firmly. I rocked my hips forward, a gasping moan escaping my mouth, breaking our kiss.

He eased back, his feral gaze intent on mine, full of heat and want and determination. He held me hard in his arms, my feet not even touching the ground. I'd never been so brazen, but I pressed my breasts closer, easing forward to capture his lips again. But he didn't let me, keeping just out of reach.

"Murgha."

"I love the way you say my name."

He set me on my feet but kept his hands firmly on me. "You're hurt." His gaze shot to my arm, his scowl deepening. "I'm sorry." He let me go abruptly and stepped away, taking his warmth with him.

Knees shaking, I sat on the stool, reeling from the erratic

sensations still buzzing through my body. I'd never felt desire like that before, not even with Dellyn. Nothing even close.

Was it because I was so desperate for someone's affection? I'd promised myself I'd only give myself to one male, the one who'd vowed himself to me. Because no male had ever even considered me worthy of more than a bedding, I never thought them worthy of my body either.

But seconds ago, all of that had flown from my mind. I was a creature of pure sensation and desire.

It wasn't as if a husband couldn't leave his wife either. That happened all the time. But I thought, at least, if my future husband and I made a vow under the gods' blessing to honor and cherish one another, then it would be harder for that male to leave me. That's why I'd made that promise to myself. I was ashamed how readily I was to forget that.

Vallon snatched the cloth off the ground and dipped it in the stream. He returned and kneeled on both knees in front of me, sighing as he pulled back the torn sleeve of my coat. "This didn't protect you much, did it?"

"The cut would've been deeper if I'd been in my own cloak."

He muttered something in demon tongue I didn't understand then pressed the ice-cold cloth to the cut. It was a jagged bone that had torn through my coat and blouse to my forearm.

"Hurt?" he asked when I winced.

"No. It feels good."

"I don't have any ointment. But we're only a few more hours from Gadlizel."

"Are you sorry you kissed me?" I blurted.

He jerked his gaze to mine, his silky black hair coasting over the exposed part of my wrist. "Why would you ask that?"

"You stopped so suddenly. I thought you might have thought it was a mistake."

"Do you think it was mistake?" he asked, his expression tight with anticipation as if my answer mattered greatly.

I considered my feelings, my emotions of relief and gratefulness that he'd saved me and dragged me out of that nightmare of a pit. But that wasn't what had made me press my lips to his. It had come from somewhere deeper. Or, perhaps, somewhere divine.

"No," I finally answered.

The tension in his face eased. "It doesn't look bad enough to need stitches, thank the gods."

"What about you?" I pushed. "Did you think it was mistake?"

He huffed out a laugh, his fangs flashing when he met my gaze. A tremble shivered through me at the sight of his teeth. I had the most outrageous desire to lick them again, feel the sharp prick of them on my tongue.

Those crimson eyes filled with the same heat of a few moments ago. "No, Murgha. It was not a mistake. It was as it should be."

When I thought he might ease forward and kiss me again, the fluttering of tiny wings announced Gwendazelle's arrival right before she landed on my knee.

"Murgha is hurt? What happened? What happened!" Her round black eyes widened with alarm.

"It's all right," I assured her.

"It was a nightwyrm."

"It attacked during the day?" She shook her little head. "Not good. Not normal."

"Indeed," said Vallon, "and they don't prey upon the fae."

"The creature was unnatural," I said, remembering how I'd sensed something odd near the dellabore bush and had followed the pulse of dark magick seeming to come right out of the ground.

"I was looking for the source of that unnatural essence, and I slipped…"

I was falling again, slipping back into the abyss, and then I could no longer see Vallon's concerned expression or Gwenda's worried one. I could see nothing at all, my mind slipping into that misty world of visions.

Of prophecy.

CHAPTER 13

VALLON

Murgha's violet eyes glazed over as she stared into the distance.

"Murgha?" I gripped her hands in mine, rubbing them to get her attention.

She didn't move or answer. Her vacant stare didn't worry me as much as it surprised me. I'd seen this happen before on seers in Gadlizel. When we once had them. King Halvar had excommunicated them all except for the very last, the one he'd slain in his great hall at the Feast of Solzkin. What should have been a time of celebration had turned into an unjust execution.

I pressed a finger to my lips as Gwenda fluttered her wings frantically, not understanding what was happening. But she sensed the magick as surely as I did. She settled and stared up at Murgha expectantly.

Murgha finally straightened her spine and spoke in a hollow voice. "Darkness is here. Very near. The demon of night speaks to many beings. Even a misguided king. He whispers of blood and massacre, of ruin and the fall. When he is set free, it will be the end of all."

Then Murgha gasped and blinked her eyes rapidly, coming back to us. I coasted my hands up her arms, squeezing lightly.

"How do you feel?" I asked her.

"Fine, I…"

"You didn't tell me you were a seer." I couldn't help the gruffness in my voice, sounding somewhat accusing.

"I've only ever had one other vision. That was years ago. I didn't know."

"You had to."

"I wasn't sure." She licked her lips nervously. "Sometimes, I get feelings about things. Like down in that den."

"What did you sense there?"

She gulped, her slender throat working. "Evil. I think that's why I had a vision now. It feels so close." She shook her head, tears pricking in her eyes. "What is wrong here in the Solgavia Mountains?"

That she innately knew something was wrong would normally have put me on guard to defend our terrible secret, the one we kept from the world in order to protect them.

I considered my loyalty to the royal family of Gadlizel, knowing that breaking any confidentiality would be breaking those vows. But Murgha was my mate. Though she didn't know it yet, she was owed my full confidence and trust. My deepest loyalty. Even above my king.

"Something I can't quite explain. Not entirely. You felt it in the den. The source of it is stirring deep in the belly of Mount Gudrun, the tallest mountain in Solgavia."

Sudden realization hit me. I stood and searched the skies, still seeing no scouts. It was nearly afternoon. They'd be circling this way soon enough.

Gwenda flew near my shoulder, her wings buzzing. "We cannot take her to Gadlizel. No, no, Vallon. We cannot."

Her black eyes were glassy with unshed tears. She tended to cry when she was afraid.

"Don't worry, my friend. I know. I agree, but we need some place safe tonight so I can figure out what to do next."

"Why can't we go to Gadlizel?" Murgha stood, stepping closer. "I don't understand what's going on."

"Gwenda, go to Windolek Castle. Speak to King Gollaya and get permission for us to visit him there."

"You can't wait here," she trilled, her voice reaching a birdlike screech.

"We're leaving now. We'll not be far behind you. But you fly faster, and we need to give the wraith king warning that a shadow fae is showing up on his doorstep. I don't want his archers to shoot us out of the sky or his dragon to eat us."

"He has a dragon?" Her expression brightened, smile widening.

"Don't flirt with his dragon, Gwenda. Just get there and get back to me."

She was gone in a streak of blue into the sky heading southwest.

Finally, I turned back to Murgha, her brow creased with a deep frown.

"I thought the dark fae didn't get along."

"They don't."

"So why are we going to see the wraith king?"

"We've met before. He's"—I couldn't think how to explain —"he's different. He may help. We helped him once when he needed it."

I didn't want to admit to her the true reason I knew he'd help me. Because the wraith king had a mate he cherished deeply and would empathize with my plight.

"Tell me what's going on," she demanded when I wouldn't answer, crossing her arms and tilting her chin up defiantly. "I'm not going anywhere with you until you explain yourself."

Closing the distance between us, I investigated her coat, realizing it wasn't as good a buy as I'd thought. It fit her well, but there were no buttons to keep it closed. It was stained from the filth of that viper's den and torn at the sleeve.

She didn't deserve to be wrapped in another woman's clothes or the homespun dress I found her in, too thin to keep her warm. She deserved better than this. It wasn't what I'd planned. But I hadn't planned to discover this fae female would be my mate either.

"The gods play tricks," I murmured as I tried to close the now soiled and tattered coat.

"That's not an answer," she snapped.

Her irritation made me smile somehow. She was fiery, my little light fae. She'd need a backbone to deal with me, that was certain. And for what lay ahead, I was afraid.

I coasted my hands around her waist, pulling her close. She flattened her hands on my chest as if to stop me, but she gave me little resistance when I lowered my head and grazed my mouth along her neck below her ear.

"We aren't going to Gadlizel because it's dangerous for you there," I informed her.

"How so?" she asked, tilting her head ever so slightly so that I could kiss her easier.

I smiled against her throat. "Seers have been banned from Gadlizel. The king considers them witches and will either kick them out of his kingdom or kill them."

Her breath hitched. "They would kill me?"

I froze. That was true fear quavering in her voice, and I would *not* have that. I lifted my head and cupped her face with both hands. "Hear me now, Murgha. You are mine to protect. And I will kill anyone who dares to try to hurt you."

Her furrowed brow rose. "Even your king?"

"*Anyone.*"

Even the prince.

The truth of it cut deep, reminding me I needed to get her out of here, and fast.

"Come. Let's pack quickly. We have to go before the night patrol circles lower into the foothills. They patrol wider during the nighttime."

I strode back to collect the portable pit and frowned at the rest of our breakfast spilled all over the ground. I wasn't a very good caregiver, it seemed. Hopefully, the wraith king would be hospitable and provide the shelter we needed while I figured out what to do next. Then she could rest and eat properly. She looked worn out from the travel and the near-death experience with the nightwyrm.

"Why do they patrol lower at nighttime?" she asked.

"To protect the world from the creatures that prowl down from the mountains in the dark."

"So the shadow fae aren't really keeping other fae out of their mountain but protecting them from what's in the mountain."

"Both."

We managed to gather our things quickly. I hooked our satchels over one arm then hoisted her into my arms. She wrapped hers around my neck easily, her expression soft and trusting.

"You're looking at me differently," I said.

"Differently how?"

"Than before."

"Well," she murmured, her gaze meeting mine, "things are different now. Aren't they?"

"That is for certain."

I bent my legs and beat my wings, leaping up and lifting off into the air, heading toward the setting sun.

CHAPTER 14

MURGHA

By the time we reached Windolek Castle, it was dark and late. Or very early.

I'd actually nodded off. The steady rhythm of his beating wings, his thumping heart beneath my cheek, and his warm embrace had lulled me to sleep. I didn't know how long we'd been flying when I felt the jolt of Vallon landing, but there were no candles or torches burning in any windows that I could see from where we were outside the wrought iron gate.

"You awake?" he asked.

"Yes," I murmured sleepily.

He set me gently on my feet and took my hand. Stepping up to the gate, he pushed me a little behind him.

"Are you Lord Vallon?" came a gruff voice on the other side of the gate.

"I am. The king is expecting us."

"Is he?" I whispered.

Vallon smiled over his shoulder, the torchlight sharpening his fine features. "Gwenda met up with us while you were sleeping."

I looked around but didn't see her. The wood sprite had a mind of her own, coming and going as she pleased. When her best friend didn't need her.

A door set in the gate swung open. "Follow me," came the guard's rough voice.

Vallon tugged me behind him. "It's all right," he assured me.

When we reached the interior of the castle, I gasped. Our entire village could've fit in the cobble-stoned bailey yard. I could see the full length of it by the line of torches leading to the castle steps beyond a set of stables for livestock.

The wraith fae in front of us had four horns and a giant build. He was no bigger than Vallon, yet he made me nervous. Most males did. Except for Vallon. How strange that was.

The wraith fae led us up the steps and inside where another guard patrolled the interior hall. He merely nodded at us and continued his vigil as we were led not into a throne room or great hall but a smaller parlor near the foot of the winding staircase.

The room was cozy with a fire burning—natural wood rather than the blue coal—several overstuffed chairs surrounding the hearth and an ornate desk set to the far side of the room, piles of parchment in neat stacks on the desk.

"Have a seat, and the king will be with you shortly," said the guard.

He left and pulled the door shut behind him, clicking a lock from the other side.

"Oh, no." I squeezed Vallon's hand, realizing I was still holding it. "They've locked us in."

"I expected it," he said casually. "The king wouldn't allow the possibility of any strangers wandering his castle with his wife and newborn child in residence."

I let go of Vallon's hand to step toward the fire and warm them.

"What makes you smile?" he asked, now beside me and watching me with that earnest intensity.

"I was just thinking of Princess Una. When I met her, we were at the beginning of war with the wraith fae. She was doing her best to assure the people that all would be well. No one knew, least of all her, how close to death she would come." I shrugged, staring into the dancing flames. "And here she is, new mother and cherished mate."

A lump suddenly formed in my throat, a stone of sadness settling in my chest.

I jumped when I felt Vallon's hand beneath my chin, tugging it up so that I would look at him.

"That makes you sad."

"Not for her." I swallowed hard. "I'm so very happy for her."

"But you fear you will never know such happiness?"

How could he see right through me, straight into my mind and divine my thoughts?

"I'm the seer, Vallon," was all I could say.

His hand on my chin coasted gently up my jaw until he was cupping my cheek. "I see you." He swept a thumb across my cheekbone, stroking gently. "And you have nothing to fear."

The door clicked and opened. Vallon dropped his hand as we both turned, but I noticed he moved his body slightly in front of me. It seemed he wasn't entirely trustful of the king. He was preparing to defend me.

I'd only ever heard stories about King Gollaya, stories of the ruthless Wraith King who had conquered Lumeria and taken the Princess of Issos into captivity, forcing her to become his concubine. Some said she was disgraced for allowing it, and she should've killed herself instead.

I never believed that. And how wrong they all were. For now, she ruled beside the greatest king in all the realms.

King Gollaya was formidable in size; all of the dark fae were. His four horns curled back in a regal swoop along his skull, his long black hair hanging loose past his shoulders. He wore a simple black shirt, unlaced at the top and dark deerskin trousers, no armor of any kind.

His casual appearance would've made me rest easier if it weren't for his penetrating gaze assessing us as we walked closer. I'd heard he had the eyes of the dragon, and so he did. Silvery-blue with a core of gold around a serpentine pupil. When he stopped in front of us, facing the firelight, they glowed with magickal luster. It was unnerving.

His magick was potent, filling up the room, making me uncomfortable. He was a zephilim, a fire wielder. And I'd heard the stories of the enemies he'd slaughtered using his god-given gift. Of what he'd done to those who'd dared to harm his queen.

"Thank you for allowing us here," Vallon said confidently.

"I must admit I was surprised when your sprite arrived with a message that you'd taken a light fae captive." His dragon-eyed gaze slid to me. "She doesn't seem too upset about her captivity."

"I'm not a captive," I blurted, growing angry at the idea of it. Then I glanced up at Vallon. "Not anymore."

Vallon's unwavering gaze melted me from the inside out. I suddenly wished the wraith king hadn't come down to meet us so quickly.

"I see," said the king.

"King Gollaya, this is Murgha. She is...with me."

The king's mouth quirked on one side. "I can see that." Then his expression turned serious. "Have a seat."

Vallon urged me into a chair closest to the fire. He sat in the one beside it, and the king took one across from us. King Gollaya eased back, lacing his clawed fingers over his abdomen, seeming casual, though I was well aware he was a deadly dark fae.

That was why Vallon wanted to come here, I realized. To seek the king's protection, a king who could kill with a word and a flicker of his magick. And for some reason, he trusted the king.

"Why have you come to Windolek?" he asked coolly.

"I had thought to take Murgha to my home in Gadlizel, but —" Vallon shifted forward in his chair, which wasn't built to accommodate wings—"circumstances have changed. I want only shelter for a few days, if you'll allow it. Then, we'll be on our way."

King Goll stared at Vallon with that piercing gaze. "Why won't she be welcome in Gadlizel? It's not because she's a light fae, or you'd not have thought to bring her there in the first place."

Vallon stiffened in his chair, staring evenly at the king. "I can't tell you."

King Goll arched a brow. "But you expect me to house you under my roof."

"I am asking it, yes. A favor."

"And how would King Halvar feel about this? His high priest hiding away with a moon fae?"

It puzzled me that he considered me a moon fae rather than a wood fae. All my life, I'd been a wood fae, the odd duckling, of course, but no one had even voiced aloud the shame of my birth and that I was not one of them. Not even Tessa.

"This doesn't concern my king."

I stared at Vallon. That wasn't entirely true. What I'd seen in my vision would affect his people. It would affect everyone if what the gods had spoken to me was true.

Vallon's gaze shifted from the king to me, unblinking and confident. I smiled at him, to tell him I was with him. If he wanted to lie to the wraith king, I wouldn't deny it. The tight brackets at his mouth softened.

"I see," said the wraith king, standing from his chair.

Vallon stood immediately as well.

"You don't have to tell me your secrets, priest. But I won't be the cause of a new war with the shadow fae."

"It would never come to that," Vallon assured him. "What I can tell you is that she would not be welcome in Gadlizel. That is the only reason. I will not put her in any danger. I only need time for a plan. And rest and refreshment for Murgha."

King Goll's gaze roamed over my torn and soiled coat before flicking back to Vallon. "I'd say you both need rest. My man will show you to your chambers. We'll talk more tomorrow, priest."

Vallon nodded. "Thank you."

King Goll strode to the door. Vallon took my hand again and guided me behind him. "Pullo," King Goll called to the wraith fae in the corridor.

The guard appeared young, his hair shaved along the sides of his head up to his four horns, his long hair braided into a tail down his back. "Sire."

"Show them to the guest chamber in the north wing. The chamber maids are there now."

So the king had already decided to give us shelter. He stopped and turned to us. "Sleep well, Vallon. And Murgha." Then he stalked up the staircase and took a right at the landing.

The one named Pullo led us to the left at the landing. We followed in silence down a darkened corridor, lit only by wall sconces. There was activity at the end of the hallway where three wraith fae females bustled out of the room with buckets, one carrying linens.

The three paused beside us, dipping into a curtsy. They all had two horns, small and delicate compared to the males.

One of them said, "A bath is ready for the lady. And the linens are fresh for you." She bobbed another curtsy, and then they continued on down the hall.

That's when it hit me that only one chamber had been prepared for us. A wash of heat flushed over my skin. Vallon smiled down at me and then pulled me by the hand toward Pullo who stood at the door.

"If you should need anything in the middle of the night, don't go wandering," he warned. "One of the king's Kel Klyss will be on guard."

I frowned up at Vallon, having never heard the term. But he simply nodded. "Understood."

Then he guided me through the door and closed it, bolting it locked behind him. That sound had my heart picking up speed, but I didn't turn to him. Instead, I wandered into the room, taking in the opulence, deciding to avoid the obvious for a moment.

"What is Kel Klyss?" I asked, still observing the room.

The castle was old, but the furnishings were not. The four-poster bed was a monstrosity, carved with intricate ivy décor, the polish shining from the fire in the hearth. The bedding was thick and plush, a deep crimson reminding me of Vallon's eyes.

"It is the king's chosen warriors. Kel Klyss is demon tongue for *the Culled*."

I stepped toward the fireplace. It was made of the obsidian known to come from the quarries near Silvantis, the royal city of Northgall. The only reason I knew that was because a peddler had come through our village with smaller stones of this kind, bartering to those who might want to make a fancy bowl or cup. The peddler had not had much luck as we were a poor village, but I'd spent time admiring the stones.

Standing in front of the mantel, I grazed my fingers over the carved filigree, wondering how big the stone must've been to carve such a piece. But then my mind went back to our conversation. "So the Culled are guards?"

"More than that. I'd say they are more like the priests of the shadow fae. A brotherhood to the king."

"But you are disobeying your king." I turned, finding Vallon directly behind me. "That's not very priestly or brotherly, is it?"

"You are correct." He stood close but didn't touch me. "My loyalty is to you now."

"Above your king?" I asked, incredulous.

"Above everyone and everything."

My heart tripped faster, that now familiar buzzing beneath my skin. Still, I asked, "Why?"

His mouth tipped slightly, those red eyes coasting over my face. "I think you should get a bath and eat, then we must talk." He nodded toward a dressing screen in the back corner.

I hadn't really noticed, but there was candlelight coming from behind it.

"It will warm you and make you feel better after the long flight." He urged me with a hand at my back.

I jumped, somewhat edgy now, then hurried toward the screen. I glanced over my shoulder, making sure he wasn't following me, but he had turned to put a new log on the fire.

Interesting that since I'd met Vallon, I'd not felt this bubbly sensation of nerves in my belly. I'd been terrified by him, then wary, then enamored, and yes, even engulfed by desire. But now... I was nervous.

I was fairly positive I knew what he hadn't admitted yet, what I felt stirring hotly in my breast. It simply couldn't be. Could it?

Once behind the screen, my entire body sighed at the sight. The large steel tub was filled with hot water and scented oils that wafted up with the steam. I also noticed laying over a chair was a beautifully made white chemise with lace along the bodice and silk ribbon ties at the shoulders. The material was thin and lovely but completely transparent.

Thankfully, there was also a jewel-green, silk dressing gown with fine embroidery in a pattern of gold-stitched flowers. It was beautiful, but more importantly, it would cover me.

I stripped quickly and eagerly lowered into the bath, unable to keep from moaning at the pleasure of the heat on my skin.

"Here you are," said Vallon, stepping around the screen with a plate of food. He'd undressed down to his shirt and trousers, his armor all gone.

"What are you doing!" I crossed my arms to cover my breasts and tucked my knees up higher.

He merely grinned and set the plate of berries, bread, and slices of cheese and cold ham on the little table next to the tub where the bath oils had also been set.

"Vallon! Get out of here," I hissed.

He completely ignored me and squatted behind me at the head of the tub. "Let's wash your hair, shall we?"

"I can do it myself."

"But I'd like to do it." He leaned over the edge and to the side at my shoulder to catch my gaze. I tucked my arms higher over my breasts, knowing full well he could see the lower half of my body. But his eyes were solely on mine. "Unless you don't want me to. I'll go away. If that's what you truly want."

Gooseflesh rose on my skin at his nearness, and when I opened my mouth to tell him that, yes, I wanted him to go away, I couldn't say the words. Because I didn't want him to go away.

"Fine," I muttered, turning to look at my pale knees sticking out of the water.

He grunted then settled behind me again. "Scoot up a little so you can dip your head back."

I huffed out a breath of annoyance but instantly did what he said. I could almost feel his arrogant smile, though I refused to look at him. Closing my eyes, I lowered my head, gripping the side of the tub so I wouldn't slip all the way under while still trying to cover my breasts with one arm.

Then Vallon's large hand gripped me by the nape and eased me down. "Relax, Murgha. I'll take care of you."

"Easier said than done," I snipped.

He chuckled, but then he started to comb through my wet hair with his other hand. I whimpered at the intense pleasure. His clawed fingers coasted lightly over my scalp.

"Feel good?" he asked.

"Heavenly," I admitted.

Tessa and I had helped wash each other's hair sometimes. It was so relaxing. Vallon's attentions weren't relaxing, however. They were arousing. No one had put their hands on me like this since...ever, really.

Dellyn's attentions had been needy and clumsy. Sadly, I was glad to have even those until I realized he only considered me worthy to be his lover. Never a partner or a wife.

Vallon poured the scented oil into my hair, smelling of some flower I didn't recognize. I wriggled my nose.

"It's from the Windolek wildflower." His voice was a silken caress as he worked the oil into my hair. "After your bath, I'll show you. The moon is up and the sky clear."

I couldn't even murmur a word as he continued to massage the oil into my hair. Then he dipped my head gently back to wash it clean. After many minutes where I drifted in the ecstasy of his hands in my hair, I felt his mouth on my forehead.

"Get dressed," he whispered, his voice husky, "and I'll show you."

When I opened my eyes, he was already gone from behind the screen, and I realized I'd gone limp and had uncovered my breasts while he'd washed my hair. I should've been embarrassed, but I wasn't. For the first time, I wanted to show another male my body, see if he found it pleasing.

I hurried with the rest of my bath and used the toweling on the chair to dry off. I wrung the water out of my hair then slipped on the chemise, the material a lovely rasp against my sensitized skin. I wrapped quickly in the robe and stepped from behind the screen, carrying the plate of food with me.

Vallon stood facing the fire, his hands clasped at his back. "Did you eat?"

"Not yet."

He turned, devouring me with his heated gaze. "Eat while I wash up."

I couldn't help but smile. "You can fit in that tub? You're awfully big."

His haughty smile returned as he walked toward me. A flush of heat crawled up my neck. I suddenly realized what he might've thought I meant about his large body and smaller, tight spaces.

"Don't you worry, darling." He cupped my face, brushing his thumbs over the slant of my cheekbones, then whispered against my lips. "I'll fit just fine." He swept a teasing, slow kiss against my lips then let me go and strode for the dressing screen.

Darling? I gulped hard, standing there stupidly with the plate in one hand. Finally, I sat by the fire and finger-combed my hair while nibbling on some of the fruit and cheese.

When I heard the splash of water, I tried *not* to imagine Vallon standing behind that screen completely naked. But I could hear the falling of water into the tub, realizing he was likely standing in the damn thing and washing his magnificent body like that.

I wondered what his broad chest looked like, his thick legs, his...everything. Sharp arousal stirred in my belly, moisture pooling between my legs. I squeezed my thighs together, trying not to listen to his sigh of pleasure as he washed in the warm water.

Gods above! I was practically hypnotized by the sound of water splashing in a tub. It was absurd.

Then I heard him shuffling from behind the screen. My hand froze with a berry halfway to my mouth. He'd wrapped the bit of toweling around his waist—and that was all he wore.

He was far more beautiful than I imagined. His sculpted chest and abdomen as well as his wings glistened from dampness. His long black hair was wet and hanging loose around his shoulders. His thick, muscular legs ended at unbelievably attractive feet, claw-tipped and all. My gaze wandered back up to the bulge between his legs, pushing against the cloth.

I gulped, but my mouth was dry as he sauntered closer, his grin telling me he knew my sad state. When he reached me, he gripped me around my wrist and lifted my hand, wrapping his warm lips around the berry still idly held between my fingers. His tongue pulled the berry free, but he took his time licking my fingertips clean.

Squeezing my thighs yet again, I couldn't prevent the moisture from coating me there.

"Mmm." His eyes danced as he chewed the berry. "Delicious."

Then he let me go and sauntered through the open double doors onto the balcony. "Come, Murgha. We have much to discuss."

CHAPTER 15

I breathed deeply, in and out, trying to cool my boiling blood. Impossible after seeing the stark desire in Murgha's eyes...for me. But we did have things to discuss first.

Sensing her sweet presence, the scent of wildflower and that quintessential smell that was her, I turned. "Come and see."

She joined me, the silky robe too long for her, dragging a little on the stone balcony. "Are your feet cold?" I asked.

She shook her head. "It's rather warm here. So different than in the mountains."

I smiled. "Even in summer, it is cold in the Solgavians."

Placing her hands on the stone banister, she looked out. Easing behind her, I cupped her delicate shoulders. She shivered then leaned back into me.

I pointed to the fields. "See them all."

"They're lovely," she said with sincerity. "They're blue?"

"Purple actually. The moonlight tints their color blue. Wait till you see them under the sunlight."

"You come over these fields often?" she asked curiously.

"As High Priest, I have many duties and errands for the royal family that take me outside of Gadlizel. I like passing over these fields in summer."

"You enjoy the beauty of nature?" She sounded disbelieving.

Squeezing her shoulder, I pressed her back against my chest and murmured against the crown of her head, "I enjoy beauty in all things."

She went quiet after that. An awkward silence stretched between us, and yet, I could smell her arousal. My demon fae instinct was to take her, and to fulfill what was my right given to me by the gods nearly overwhelmed me into action. But I wouldn't until she understood.

"Aren't you going to ask?" I finally offered into the quiet.

"Ask you what?" Her voice trembled.

I smiled at her pretense. "Why I would put your welfare above everything else. A high priest of Gadlizel doesn't switch allegiance on a whim."

"It was your father's dying wish. You said that vows on the deathbed are considered sacred."

"They are. But it wouldn't make me abandon my vows to the royal family of Gadlizel."

"Then why are you?"

Gently, I turned her to face me, finding a myriad of emotions flitting across her face—fear, wonder, hope.

"Because you are my mate."

There was no surprise on her face, but her eyes narrowed as she finally spoke with defiance. "That can't be true."

"Why not?"

"Because you're a shadow fae, and I'm a light fae half-breed. The gods would not tie us together."

I coasted my hands to her throat, tipping her chin up with my thumbs when she tried to look away. "Are you disgusted by being with me?"

"No!" she exclaimed quickly. "It just doesn't seem right. It doesn't make sense."

"It does to me."

She stared, unblinking, her violet eyes bluer under the moonlight, just like the wildflowers. Utterly enchanting. I wanted to sweep her into my arms and show her the pleasure of a mated couple. I'd only heard about it through others, the complete joy of sharing your body with a god-given mate.

I yearned for it, but she needed to accept what we were first. Because after I took her to bed and sank my fangs into her flesh and my cock into her body, she would be mine forever.

"So the gods just tell us who we must be with," she snapped angrily. "We have no choice."

"Perhaps the gods already know who we will choose because they're gods," I offered calmly. "Rather than choosing for us, they simply help us along by showing us."

"Show us how?"

"With the marks on our hearts." I took her wrist and placed her palm over my heart. "I feel it here," I said, hearing my voice drop darkly. "Every time you're near me. Even when you're not." I searched her face intently. "I could've kept my vow to my father by sending a shadow guard to watch over you. I could've done my duty without ever laying eyes on you." I shook my head. "But something pulled me down out of the mountains."

"What did?"

"You."

I pressed my hand over the left side of her chest, engulfing half her breast. "Don't you feel me in here?"

"Yes," she said without hesitation, her eyes wide and wild.

"Don't you want me in here?"

"More than anything. I want you everywhere." She closed her eyes for a second then opened them and licked her lips, her voice shaky when she added, "But I made a promise to myself. I would only give my body to one male. My husband."

"Then marry me here under the moonlight and let me make you mine, sweet Murgha."

She scoffed. "Marry you here?"

"Why not? Do you need witnesses?"

"No, but—" She shook her head. "Weddings take time and planning."

"I don't need a ceremony. The vows are between you and me and the gods. Don't light fae marry under Lumera's light?"

She glanced up at the moon. Lumera, the Goddess of the Moon, was the favored goddess of the moon fae.

"We do. With a handfasting and request for the Goddess of the Wood's blessing as well."

"Then so be it. Tell me what to say, and I will say it."

She laughed again. "And just like that, we will be husband and wife?" Her expression was still disbelieving.

"If you will have me, Murgha," I added softly, picking up her palm from my chest and pressing a kiss to the center of her palm. "Will you put me out of my misery and become my wife?"

Her brow puckered into a frown. "What misery?"

It was my turn to huff a laughter of disbelief. "Being near you without having you is sheer torture. Don't you understand that?"

When I thought she would deny it, she said simply, "Yes. I understand."

Clenching my jaw, I wrapped a hand around her waist. "Then marry me. Right now."

She searched my face, finding only sincere honesty there, for that is all that I felt. "What about shadow fae? How do you marry?"

I dropped my head back, laughing toward the sky.

"What?"

I met her gaze, finding that intensely curious expression I adored. "It's not as civilized as light fae mating ceremonies." Though ours wasn't as barbaric as the wraith fae's either.

"Tell me," she demanded.

Staring into those fathomless pools, I said, "The shadow fae prefer private ceremonies between only the couple. We fly high up into the Solgavia peaks and beneath the sun god Solzkin's light, we pledge ourselves to each other."

"With certain words?"

"Yes. But it isn't the words that bind us." She remained silent, waiting, so I continued. "It is the bite the male leaves on her throat." I pointed to the base of mine to show her where. "And we consummate our binding in the open air beneath the sun."

I waited for a look of revulsion but found the opposite. A flicker of desire darkened her eyes.

"Let's do it your way," she said with confidence. "Beneath Lumera's light." Her gaze drifted to the moon then back to me while my heart tried to pound through my ribcage and out of my chest.

"You want to marry me in the shadow fae way?" I asked to be sure I heard her correctly.

"Yes. With the blessing of Lumera's light, we will combine our faiths of dark and light. Since we are both, the binding should be both." She blinked nervously. "Don't you agree?"

"I agree."

Unable to wait a moment longer, I reached for the tie of her robe then loosened it slowly. Her hands clenched into fists at her side, but she didn't protest. Easing the robe open, I slid it off her shoulders and let it pool on the cool stone beneath our feet.

By the gods, she was lovely. Achingly beautiful.

Her body was sweetly made. Her small breasts with tight pink peaks pressed against the sheer lace of the shift's bodice. Her hips flared wide, which made me grunt in pleasure. It would be easier for her to take me and to bear my children.

I pulled the ribbons at her shoulders, letting the shift fall next, revealing her entirely to me. Swallowing hard, I pulled the toweling from my waist and dropped it aside. Her gaze lowered, taking me in, her mouth falling open before she squeezed her eyes shut then looked back up at me.

"How does it work?" she asked, voice quivering.

"I'll give you my vows. Then you give me yours. That comes first."

She nodded, so I took her small hands in mine and stepped closer, ignoring the painful erection between us.

"Murgha," I began softly, "I pledge you my life and my heart from this day forward. I will protect you and keep you safe always. Beneath Lumera's light, I give you my love till my dying breath."

She stared wonderingly, her eyes glassy with unshed tears. "Love?"

"Yes." I nodded. "Love."

"How can you speak of love? We only just met. You don't even know me."

A laugh rumbled in my chest. "I know that your kind, giving spirit will warm me on many cold nights. I know that your curious nature makes me smile. And I know that your tender, loving heart is worth cherishing. It's worth fighting for." I pressed my forehead to hers. "My heart began beating only for you since the moment I saw you in that inn. If that isn't love, then I don't know what is."

Tears streaked down her cheeks then fell away. I stepped back, waiting for her vows.

She licked her lips and lifted her chin, holding my gaze. "Vallon of House Hennawyn, I promise to care for you, to be faithful, and to..."—she paused, her heart in her eyes—"and to *love* only you from now and into the afterworld. I ask for Elska's blessing beneath Lumera's light to shine upon us with the gifts of marriage—enduring companionship, children if the gods wish it, and steadfast loyalty. I will never abandon you or our marriage."

This was important to her. Her mother had essentially abandoned her husband when she'd fallen for her true father. And though the mating bond was strong enough to lure her mother into infidelity, it obviously placed a mark on my Murgha. For her mother had abandoned her as well, leaving her with a parent who wasn't truly hers and who didn't truly love her.

"And I will never abandon you," I vowed.

Then I pressed my mouth to hers, sealing our vows with a tender kiss.

CHAPTER 16

MURGHA

The night was warm, and yet I couldn't stop shaking, my body buzzing with anticipation and my heart about to burst at what I was doing.

I wasn't the rash sister. Tessa was. I'd always thought through every action with careful scrutiny. But here I was, giving my entire self to a shadow fae I met two days ago. My logical mind was reeling from what I was doing, while my heart urged me forward and my soul rejoiced.

Vallon stared into my eyes, coasting his warm palms from my bare shoulders and down my arms, then he lowered himself to his knees, his wings flaring wide. I watched as he kissed and nipped across my belly to my hip, too aroused to be embarrassed.

He lowered to his haunches, his hands trailing up my thighs and around to my backside.

"Come closer," he urged, tugging me forward.

I wasn't entirely ignorant of the sexual act, but I didn't quite understand what he wanted until he slid both thumbs through my thatch of curls, spread the lips of my sex and opened his warm mouth on the tight bud between.

"Ah!" I cried out, grabbing hold of his shoulder and one of his horns at the same time.

He lapped and licked, drawing out spikes of pleasure with every sweep of his long tongue.

"Vallon," I whispered, squirming beneath the heavenly sensation.

Growling against my clitoris, which only made me moan louder, he lifted one of my legs and draped it over his shoulder, opening me wider.

"I can't...oh, gods." I gripped his horn tight and rocked my pussy against his mouth, writhing with the hot pleasure pouring through my body.

He held my thigh hard, keeping me balanced as he laved and sucked then tongued inside me, driving my arousal toward a spiraling peak.

I ground harder against his mouth, whimpering with the luxurious heat climbing higher, making me hotter.

"Yes, Vallon," I hissed, feeling my climax spin higher, closer. "Just like that. Yes!"

My head dropped back, and I cried out with a shout when my orgasm burst wide, ecstasy engulfing me. While my body still hummed with pleasure, Vallon stood and lifted me by the waist.

"Wrap your legs around me," he commanded gruffly.

I did, feeling the broad length of his cock rub against my slick sex. He had one arm around my waist, the other hand wrapping my nape.

"This may hurt the first time." His breaths were coming fast, but his body was solid and strong.

"I don't mind," I said dreamily, still high on the sublime climax and of being claimed by my mate. "I think I'd like a little pain," I added, not even sure where the words came from. "It will help me remember this night."

With a rough sound, he maneuvered me until his cock was at my entrance. His crimson eyes were nearly full black, swamped by his dilated pupils, by his heady desire.

Then he sank his cock in slowly, a long purring growl vibrating in his chest. I gasped at the tight intrusion, a sharp sting as he thrust deeper, and then he was buried fully inside me.

My mouth open, I panted through the pain. He waited, watching me with those unfathomable feral eyes.

"Do you see?" he asked in that silky voice, nipping at my bottom lip with his teeth. "You were made for me." Another nip, this one sharper, then he leaned forward and whispered in my ear, "This tight cunt is mine, Murgha."

He began to move, slowly dragging his thick cock out. I whimpered, gripping him around the shoulders.

"Your sweet cunt has been waiting for me," he growled on a deep thrust.

"Ah!"

He dragged his mouth down my throat, fisting my hair loosely and tugging my head back.

"I need to feel you to come. Need to feel you squeeze my cock." He began to thrust deeper, harder.

I fell back, but his wings wrapped around me, holding me in place.

"I'm going to fill you up, little mate, but not until you come again."

I might've marveled at how he was standing up and holding me while he thrusted so hard and deep, like I weighed nothing, but my mind was lost to the euphoric sensation of being filled by him.

He reached between us and mounded my breast, his claws lightly scraping my skin, and then he squeezed my nipple, careful not to scratch me.

"Yes," I murmured, gripping one of his horns again. "That feels good."

He grunted and hiked me up, his cock pulling free.

"No," I gasped, but then he was sucking my nipple, tonguing and twirling, nipping with a little fang. "Gods, Vallon. Please!"

I rocked my soaked sex against his abdomen, needing him back inside me. In a flash, he opened his wings and spun me in his arms, setting me gently down on my feet facing the balcony.

"Hands on the banister," he ordered. "Hold on."

I barely had a grip before he thrust his cock all the way inside me with one pump. Again, I moaned, unsure my legs would hold me up. But Vallon gripped my fleshy hips and drove inside me with deep, grinding thrusts, lifting me onto my toes.

The wet sound of sex with each drive of his cock, my moans, his groans, and all under the open night sky dragged me into a sensory vortex.

"Please, Vallon! So close."

He pounded faster, sliding a hand between my legs and circling my clitoris with the pad of his finger.

"Come for me, Murgha," he growled close to my ear, his wings wrapping around us yet again. "Let me feel your pleasure squeezing my cock."

Then I was, screaming and coming, barely feeling the pain when he sank his fangs at the curve of my neck and shoulder. The prick of his bite only made my pussy pulse harder. He growled, sucking and licking as he drove in one last time, his cock emptying deep inside me.

"Yes," he groaned, holding me hard and grinding against my buttocks. "Mine." His voice was no longer velvety and silky, but beastly and dark. "You are fucking *mine*," he repeated, dragging his cock out to the tip and pounding in once more, still spilling his seed inside me.

I'd never felt so wonderfully used, my body throbbing with both pain and pleasure. Vallon remained buried inside me as he lapped at the wound in my neck, a low purring sound vibrating from his chest to my back.

But then, the gentle Vallon suddenly returned as he hauled my torso back against him, still deep inside me when he whispered, "I'll never let you go, Murgha." He nuzzled my cheek. "I'll never abandon you."

A wave of emotion washed through me, drawing tears from my eyes. I hadn't known how badly I needed those words. Even more, I believed them with my whole heart to be true.

Then Vallon finally pulled from inside me, scooped me into his arms, and carried me to bed. I was already half asleep when I felt him wiping a warm cloth between my legs. When he pulled the covers over us both and curled his body behind mine, I fell immediately into a dreamless sleep.

CHAPTER 17

VALLON

I woke with a jolt. I heard nothing, saw no intruder. Nevertheless, a shadow fae was near. I felt his magick, a ghostly whisper along my skin.

Silently, I reached for my knife beside the bed, unsheathing it without making a sound. A quick scan of the room. He wasn't in here. The curtains billowed at the open balcony door, larks chirping in the early light of morning.

I stepped cautiously outside, ready for an attack, looking toward the shadows where he'd likely hid himself with magick. But then I saw the intruder, not hiding at all.

He stood to the far left of our balcony, back straight and rigid, looking out toward the mountains, the first light of dawn shining on his golden hair. Rather than relax, I remained ready to defend should I need to.

"My prince," I acknowledged.

He turned slowly, taking in my nakedness and my fighting stance. "My prince? So formal, Vallon. It is just us." There was a twinge of hurt in his voice.

I didn't answer. I was far from where I was supposed to be, sleeping in the wraith king's castle, which was unheard of. Last I reported to him, I was on watch in the woods south of Lake Moreen, checking on my ward. Torvyn knew all about my father's dying wish.

But now, I was miles away from our home, where I should have been. And no doubt, he could smell her on me.

He stared, his golden eyes taking everything in as always. "She's pretty, your little ward."

"She's my mate," I snapped quickly. "My wife."

For the first time since I'd known him as a boy, a look of shock widened his eyes. "That is...unexpected."

"Nevertheless, it is true." Tension vibrated from my frame, and I still clenched my knife at my side.

"No one will care if the high priest takes a light fae to wife." He glanced at the blade in my hand. "Is that why you've hidden away with her in King Goll's summer castle?"

"There are other reasons I cannot bring her to Gadlizel."

"What reasons?" As always, his question wasn't a question. It was a command.

As high priest, I usually answered without pause. But now, I kept my mouth closed.

The sun peaked above the horizon, gilding his orange-tipped black wings, the markings of his royal line.

"Why are you threatened by me?" he asked, a frown pursing his brow. "We're friends."

"Are we?" I couldn't keep the gruff tone out of my voice.

"What are you talking about? Of course, we are."

"Torvyn, you've been withdrawing more and more these past

many months. Even when I see you or talk to you, I feel like you're not truly there. I fear that—" I cut off my own words, refusing to say what I believed. But Torvyn's dawning expression said he knew.

"That I'm turning into my father."

I nodded stiffly.

He heaved a sigh and looked out at the mountains. "I am not mad, Vallon. I'm angry and frustrated, and I'm fucking *frightened*." His voice had dropped to a whisper.

I'd never heard him admit the last. He was certainly speaking to me as his friend now.

"We all are," I admitted, for the evil was waking with rapid speed and slowly bleeding out into the world.

"So that's why you won't bring your little wife to Gadlizel? Too close to the monster we're fighting?"

"It isn't that actually," I admitted. For though it was true the evil being that lived deep in the mountain was growing in strength, I knew I could protect her. I'd flee the mountain with her at the first sign the dark one had broken through our wards.

"Then tell me, brother."

I startled. Torvyn hadn't used that term of affection in years. When we were boys, we would pretend we were brothers since both of us had no siblings. By all accounts, with the exception of a blood bond, we were. We'd lived through many trials together, but this past year he'd withdrawn. And that was what had me cautious about telling him.

"She is a seer," I said flatly.

His frown deepened. "What kind?"

"A world seer."

There were three kinds. A soul seer prophesied only for one person and their future. These seers were always attached to people of importance, usually kings or queens. God seers spoke the will of one of the gods. But a world seer saw visions that impacted all of fae kind.

"I see," said Torvyn.

"Exactly. I won't bring her to Gadlizel because she'd be in more danger from your father than from what lies in the belly of the mountain."

He turned back to face the sunrise. I joined him at the banister, setting my blade on the flat of the stone railing.

"I understand your hesitance, but I need you, Vallon."

"I'd kill anyone who tried to harm her," I admitted, "including your father."

He turned his head to me, observing the truth written on my face. "Then she is your god-given mate."

"She is."

"So we don't tell anyone she's a seer," he said conspiratorially.

Suddenly, I felt as if I was speaking to my friend like we always had. He and I against the rest of the world.

"You'd hide that truth from your father in defiance of his law?"

"My father." He snorted. "I barely recognize him from the man he once was, Vallon. You know it as well as I do."

Yes, I did. The king was not the man I had pledged my fealty to so many years ago.

"What if she has a vision among others?" I asked. "She doesn't have control of her magick yet."

"Vallon, you never come to court now, and your villa is so far above Gadlizel, you might as well live in a different realm. No one will think it strange that you rarely come to court since it has always been so with you."

"I prefer my solitude," I said flatly.

He chuckled, a sound I hadn't heard in a long while, but then he sobered, his golden eyes sincere when he said, "I need you, brother. I'll protect your mate as well. I give you my solemn vow." He held out his hand, forearm vertical. "Besides," he added, "perhaps she was put into your life to help us all. A world seer, Vallon? It's rather coincidental, don't you think?"

"I think it's the gods' doing."

"Then let us listen to the gods. Just because my father ignores them doesn't mean that I do." He opened his palm. "Take my hand. Take my oath."

I pressed my forearm to his and clasped his hand, relief and rightness washing through me. "I accept your vow to protect my mate with your life." I held his gaze, finding only the loyalty of my dearest friend.

"With my life," he agreed.

I exhaled a breath with sharp relief as I clasped his shoulder with my free hand. "I've missed you, Torvyn."

"I am sorry I've been so"—he huffed out a breath—"removed." He glanced down and dropped my arm. "Now, as much as I enjoy standing here while you're naked, you should probably return to your wife."

I laughed and stepped away, taking my blade from the banister.

"When can I expect you back home?" he asked, opening his wings, readying for flight.

"Soon. We have an errand first that will take a few days. But don't come calling for a week. Or two. Perhaps three."

He laughed again, a warm sound that reminded me of our carefree days of youth. There was little cause for joy or laughter these days in Gadlizel. It was good to hear the lightness in his voice.

"I'll give you a full cycle of the moon, then be ready for my visit." He flapped his wings once and landed atop the railing.

"What are you going to do about your mother? She may be in the way for all the recreation you have planned with your new bride."

"My mother will be overjoyed and will stay well out of the way because she's wanted grandchildren for ages."

That suddenly struck me. The idea of children with Murgha. My heart clenched with warmth.

"Quite right," said my friend, the Prince of Gadlizel. "See you in a month."

Then he lifted off and sped high into the sky. I noticed a larger shadow streaking through the clouds high above us. The king's dragon. On patrol, most likely. But with a shimmer of light, Torvyn vanished, camouflaged with the sky. The dragon might smell him on the wind, but he'd never see him.

I returned to the bedchamber to find Murgha still peacefully asleep. Her lovely face upturned toward the morning light, the covers tucked under her slender arm across her breasts, completely unaware of what had transpired. There was so much I had to tell her about Gadlizel. But not now.

I'd tell her later. Instead, I sank back under the covers behind her and pulled her warm body against mine, relishing this bliss before we had to return to the world.

CHAPTER 18

MURGHA

I STOOD BENEATH THE SOLITARY TREE ON THE PLAIN, ITS BRANCHES shielding me from the afternoon sun while we waited outside of Vanglosa, the main encampment of the largest clan of beast fae in Northgall.

"What if it isn't her?" I asked nervously.

Vallon stood directly behind me, comforting hands on my shoulders. "Do you honestly believe there is more than one wood fae named Tessa mated to a beast fae?"

"You're right." I laughed at my own silliness. "It's her."

The beast fae scout who stopped us from moving farther into their encampment readily admitted there was someone matching my sister's description and name living with her mate in Vanglosa. After scowling at Vallon and telling us to stay put, he mounted his Meer-wolf, a terrifying giant gray beast, and galloped back toward their camp.

They didn't live in permanent stone or wood structures. Their village was made up of deer-hide tents. But the village was much larger than I'd anticipated.

Two Meer-wolves with riders emerged from Vanglosa, moving at a steady, but not hurried, clip. Neither was the scout who told us to stay where we were.

As they drew closer, I stiffened at the sight of the two beast fae males on the backs of two Meer-wolves—one a dark gray, the other was black and bigger.

I'd heard of the giant wolves who lived in Northgall. Everyone had. They were often companions of the beast fae, the only fae who could tame the mammoth wild creatures.

But it was the two beast fae riding the wolves who caught my attention. Vallon rumbled a growl and pulled me tighter against him.

"Who is that?"

"The Lord of the Beast Fae and his chief warrior."

"Why are you all agitated?" Besides the obvious fact that they were the largest fae I'd ever laid eyes on.

"I don't like the beast lord. He's...difficult."

"You've had dealings with him before?"

He scoffed. "Not dealings. More like received multiple warnings. He's not friendly."

We waited silently as they drew closer. Both of them dismounted just beyond the tree. They were both wearing only a hide skirt, demon runes tracking across their broad chests and muscular arms. Both had four, thick spiraling horns. One had silver bands at the base of his horns, the other one—the bigger one—wore gold. Their king.

The chief warrior had black hair and a cool expression, though there was a slight pinch between his brows as he studied me. His yellow eyes practically glowed in the afternoon light. His skin was a tawny brown. The beast lord's complexion was a deeper shade of bronze, his brown hair shining with auburn highlights in the sun.

Their faces were...unusual. Their jaws were wide, sharp, and square, the noses and mouths jutting forward more than seemed natural. Their foreheads were prominent, holding the largest sets of spiraling horns I'd ever seen. And though their facial features indeed matched more beastly features than fae, I couldn't help but think them strangely handsome. Formidable, powerful fae.

They had no wings like the shadow fae of course, but they both had long tails covered in a fine pelt, tipped with coarse hair. Actually, their bodies were covered in more hair than most fae. I tried not to stare, but it was rather impossible.

The beast lord crossed his arms, his huge biceps bulging, his tail flicking back and forth behind him.

"Lord Redvyr," said Vallon in greeting. "Chief Bezaliel."

"What do you want?" asked Lord Redvyr, his deep voice rough and harsh.

No niceties at all then.

"My mate wishes to see her sister who is living with your clan," Vallon said since I couldn't seem to get a word out of my mouth.

Lord Redvyr lifted his nose to the air and inhaled, settling his eerie orange eyes on me. He appeared like a very large cat waiting to pounce.

He grunted. "You couldn't find one of your own, priest? Had to poach on the wood fae?"

Vallon stiffened, his hands curling tighter at my shoulders.

"The gods have bound us to each other," I said, finally finding my voice. "He did not steal me."

Well, at first, he did. But I decided not to mention that.

Lord Redvyr's gaze turned back to me. He arched a superior

brow. And while he appeared much less civilized than most fae, I sensed the superiority of his strength and power.

"It's unnatural," said the beast lord. "A tiny little wood fae mating with one of those creatures."

I wanted to laugh, that the beast lord saw Vallon as a *creature*, not a fae, when most of the world saw the beast fae as the most different of our kind.

"Red," snapped the chief, his tail now twitching with agitation.

Redvyr rolled his eyes and uncrossed his arms. He then propped one hand on the fierce-looking black wolf standing beside him and the other low on his hip as he continued to study us.

"Those things need to stay on their mountain," he told his chief.

Anger boiled up inside me at his insult. "Are you prejudiced against fae mating another not of their own kind, my lord, or do you simply hate the shadow fae?"

The beast lord's orange eyes narrowed, his tail flicking more, then he smiled, revealing how long and sharp his canines were. "Feisty little wood fae. Maybe she is her sister."

"She is," said the chief. "She matches her description."

"So my sister *is* living with you." I tried to take a step forward, but Vallon's grip tightened, keeping me close to him. "Please. You have to let me see her."

"You can come, but he cannot," said Redvyr.

"She goes nowhere without me." Vallon had said very little and protested not at all until now.

Redvyr stared at Vallon, raising the hairs on my arms at the inherent threat there. Then he whistled loudly over his shoulder.

At once, another Meer-wolf, a pale gray smaller one, came

trotting out of the encampment. As it drew closer, I could make out its rider, my heart racing with sheer joy.

"Tessa," I whispered, tears pricking my eyes.

I broke free from Vallon's hold and ran toward her. She stopped the wolf and slid off carefully, a bundle wrapped around her shoulders and waist. Then she was running toward me, laughing and crying like I was.

"Tessa!" I screamed, sprinting across the tall grass of the plain.

We collided and wrapped around each other, but just as quickly I drew back at the gurgling grunt of an infant between us.

"Oh, Murgha, let me look at you." She cupped my cheeks, smiling through tears.

But I was staring at the child swaddled in a sling crossing one of her shoulders. "Tessa," I panted breathlessly. "Is this babe yours?"

She was still staring at me with all the love I'd missed, but then she laughed and tugged open the cloth hiding her child.

"Saralyn, meet your Aunt Murgha."

I peered beneath the swaddle at the most beautiful brown-skinned, dark-haired baby girl. Her eyes were wide and hazel, lashes thick and dark, the nubs of horns showing beneath her hair.

"Oh, Tessa." I sniffed at the onslaught of emotion. "May I hold her?"

"Let's sit down." Tessa sat cross-legged, tugging on my arm to follow.

I did. She untied the sling from around her shoulders, lowering the sweet baby into her lap, then she lifted her gently toward me.

In utter shock and disbelief, I held the precious bundle close to my chest. "My niece," I whispered, staring at her beautiful, little face.

She cooed back sweetly, then a tiny tail wrapped around my wrist.

"Oh!" I gasped.

Tessa laughed. "I know. Takes some getting used to. She likes to grab hold of everything with her tail."

I shook my head, laughing softly. "So you were telling the truth in the letter you left on the inn doorstep."

Tessa was combing a hand through my hair, a sign of her affection. "Yes." Her voice sobered. "You thought I was forced, didn't you?"

"I did," I confessed. "What else was I supposed to think, Tessa? You'd gone into the woods for juniper and never returned."

"I know, I know." She took my free hand and squeezed. "I'm sorry." Her gaze drifted over my shoulder. "Are you truly here with a shadow fae?"

"I am. He's my husband."

It was her turn to look shocked. "What!"

Smiling, I arched a brow. "Is it so hard to believe? You mated with a beast fae, after all."

"It's just...how in the name of the gods did that happen? How did you meet a shadow fae?"

"It's a long story." And a sad one, which I wasn't ready to tell. I wanted to bask in the bliss of this moment. "I'll tell you later." I stared down at the sweet face peering up at me. "Right now, I want to simply hold my darling niece and hear all about your new life here."

So Tessa told me of her adventures as mate to a beast fae, moving to new camps, enjoying a carefree kind of life. They didn't worry about working for coin or trading with others to make it through the winter. They all worked together to provide for the clan, living harmoniously. Well, relatively so. She said there was still the same old jealousy as in any clan.

Her mate was the chief warrior I'd just met, Bezaliel. Tessa hadn't been welcomed at first, having taken and claimed one of their finest warriors to be her own. Of course, he'd ensured everyone knew that she was now part of their clan, no matter that she was born a wood fae. It gave me hope that I'd find some harmony in my new life in Gadlizel.

I'd noted that Vallon, Bezaliel, and Redvyr had drawn closer to us, but kept far enough away to give us privacy. I'd even seen them speaking to Vallon. Since they weren't at blows, I assumed it was somewhat civil.

I'd been stroking Saralyn along the soft tuft of hair between the nubs of her horns when a familiar buzzing caught my attention.

Gwendazelle landed on my knee, gasping with wide-eyed wonder. "Oh, look, look, my lady. A sweet, sweet baby."

"What—?" Tessa looked frightened, about to shoo her away.

"It's all right. She's my friend," I assured Tessa.

Saralyn's eyes snapped open. She laughed and cooed, reaching her tail up to brush Gwenda's wing.

"I love sweet babies," Gwenda's high-pitched voice trilled. "I can't wait till you have one, my lady." She blinked shyly at me.

Tessa's expression turned serious again. "So you'll live up in the Solgavias with him?"

"Yes."

"Be careful." Tessa gripped my hand again, giving it a squeeze. "Bezaliel says there's something stirring in the mountains. Something very bad."

If she only knew, but I'd promised Vallon we would keep my prophecy to ourselves for now. We'd see if the gods would give us more guidance.

There was a reason the gods saw fit that Vallon and I should find one another. My place was with him in Gadlizel. My purpose was greater than I could've ever imagined when I was with Papa in the inn.

I could help the shadow fae. All faekind. I would. I knew it down to my soul.

"I know, Tessa," I finally answered, squeezing her hand back. "Do not worry. I am well-protected."

My gaze slid to my left where Vallon stood, his wings flared, silhouetted against the sinking sun. My heart was full. For no matter what was in store, I knew I was exactly where the gods wanted me to be.

EPILOGUE

MURGHA

"You're going to kill me," Vallon growled, staring down at me as I took his cock deeper down my throat.

As much as I enjoyed the pleasure Vallon had given to me nightly since we'd returned to his villa above Gadlizel, I found a particular kind of joy in making him unravel. Like now.

Though I couldn't swallow him completely, I always tried, and he appeared both tortured and enraptured by my attempts.

Moaning, I sucked him to the tip and swirled my tongue around his engorged head. His jaw clamped as he held my nape gently.

"One more time. Suck me deep."

Smiling, I opened my mouth and relaxed my throat, allowing him to sink partially down as I breathed through my nose.

His eyes were full black as he swept his thumb over my top lip where it stretched around his cock.

"The only thing I love more than fucking this pretty mouth is fucking your sweet cunt."

In a quick move, he pulled out of my mouth, lifted me beneath my arms, and tossed me back onto our bed. I was still wearing one of the new chemises he'd bought me—a pretty, lacy thing. But I heard it tear when he jerked the hem up hastily, curling his arms beneath my knees and spreading me wide.

His heated gaze was focused down below as he lined his cock at my entrance and sank inside me on a shuddering groan. I was slick and ready, as always.

"So wet," he murmured against my mouth before kissing me.

I fisted my hand in his hair and tugged, knowing he liked it when I let myself go. "Some of that is from my mouth," I teased.

A growl rumbled in his chest. "This sweet, fucking mouth." He kissed along my jaw to my throat. "And the honey from your cunt." He nipped at my shoulder. "I could eat you alive."

I laughed, but then he angled and hit me deeper. "Gods, I'm coming already."

"Yes, my love." He hammered harder. "Let me feel you come on my cock."

As always, his dirty mouth and perfect thrusting sent me right over the edge. I screamed, arching my neck as I came. He bent his head and sucked my nipple into his mouth. My sex squeezed him as my climax seized my entire body.

He grunted, holding himself deep while grinding inside me. "Feels so fucking good."

I whimpered as he sat back on his heels, his cock still inside me then he circled his thumb around my sensitive nub.

"No," I reached down, trying to bat him away.

"Shh." He grabbed my wrist and continued to circle my clitoris, massaging slowly. "I want another one before I fill you up."

That feral, fiery red gaze stared hotly down at me, while I squirmed on his cock, completely in his thrall.

"I don't think I can," I protested, feeling completely boneless.

"Hands above your head," he commanded. "Hold onto the headboard."

There were small slats carved into the headboard that happened to be the perfect width for me to grasp.

"Hands up," he ordered again more gruffly when I didn't move. "And keep them there."

I gripped the headboard slats, jutting my breasts upward. They caught his gaze. He groaned, reaching up one hand to pinch my nipple, rolling it between thumb and middle finger, his claws lightly scraping.

"Ah," I cried out, my sex squeezing again, the warmth of arousal building instantly.

There was something about the gentle caress of those deadly claws on my skin that always stirred my arousal. While he pinched and twisted my tight nipples till they stung, he then dragged his claws lightly over my breasts, scraping the sensitive peaks.

"Vallon," I whispered, rocking my hips.

"There it is." His gaze dropped then he rolled my clitoris with the pad of his thumb, spreading the new slick over it. "More honey for me, eh, darling?"

"Stop teasing me." I bent my knees higher and planted my feet on his chest. "Fuck me, Vallon."

His eyes blazed wildly. He loved it when I told him what to do in bed.

He hissed as he stared down where our bodies were joined, his cock swelling bigger inside me. He grabbed my hips and did as I asked, thrusting with long, deep pumps.

"Like that?" He squeezed my hips tighter, his claws pricking my flesh. "You want a hard fucking, darling?"

"Harder," I panted, holding on tight to the headboard. "Faster."

"*Gods*, Murgha."

Then he fucked me with the animalistic fervor I relished. I loved when he was tender, but gods save me, I loved it more when he fucked me good and hard.

"Yes!" I felt my breasts bouncing with each hard pound of his hips. "Just like that."

He growled, his red eyes holding me captive as he drove inside me over and over. "*Yes*," he groaned as my pussy began to pulse with my second climax. "That's what I wanted." He continued pounding me even as I came, my mouth falling open on another cry. "Your sweet cunt squeezing me hard."

Suddenly, he arched his neck, dropping his head back as he roared, pounding with one last deep thrust, holding my hips off the bed as he spilled inside me. I smiled at the glorious picture he made, releasing his seed, completely undone.

As he slowly came down from his own climax, I coasted one foot up his shoulder and flicked his pointed ear with my toe.

He finally looked down at me, grinning like the demon he was. He pressed a kiss to my ankle then took hold of both and wrapped my legs at his waist as he lowered down to me, still buried to the hilt.

While he held his weight on his forearms, I smoothed my hands over his chest, noticing the scratches I'd left last night and the—

"Oh, no." I touched the bite mark on his bicep. "I bit you last night."

He grinned, flashing his sharp, white fangs. "I know. I love it when you mark me up."

"Your mother is going to think I'm a wild barbarian."

He chuckled and swept a lock of hair away from my face, running his pad along my cheek. "My mother is overjoyed that she might live to be a grandmother. She'd all but given up."

I smiled. I loved Vallon's mother. Meera was a lovely older shadow fae with long silvery hair and the kindest eyes. I was shocked how quickly we'd bonded when I first came last month. She didn't seem to care that I was a light fae or a half-breed moon and wood fae. She only cared that I was her son's wife.

"You put a smile on his heart," she'd told me one night while we sat by the fire. "That's all a mother could ask for."

I stared up at Vallon and coasted my fingers through his silky hair falling like a black curtain around my face.

"So you didn't have lots of potential shadow fae women lining up to be the lady of House Hennawyn?"

He lowered further, his smile turning teasing. "Plenty wanted the role, but I never let them get even close."

"Why not?"

"Because none were my mate. I knew that I was destined for a true binding, for mated bliss, for deep love." His expression shifted more seriously as he swept a gentle kiss against my mouth.

"And you found it," I said with confidence.

"Indeed. I have." Another soft kiss as he ground inside me. "And how about you, Lady Murgha of House Hennawyn? Have you found that deep love and happiness?"

My pulse leaped at the tender question, for he truly needed to hear it. "I have, Vallon. With all my heart."

We kissed tenderly for quite a long time. When his cock began to harden again, he pulled from inside me.

"Oh." I squeezed my thighs shut as he hopped out of bed. "Where are you going?"

"Time to get dressed. We have company coming today."

"Who?" I sat up, holding the covers to my breasts.

"The Prince of Gadlizel. He sent a messenger yesterday, giving us warning that he'd be visiting today."

I hurried out of bed and pulled my dressing gown on. "Is it a special occasion?"

Vallon tied the lacings of his trousers then stalked toward me. "Yes." He cupped my face. "He wants to meet his best friend's new wife. And the seer."

I placed my palms over the backs of his hands. "You're sure he won't kick me out or anything? Because of the king's laws."

"No one will touch you." His voice deepened. "I promise you that."

"There's something else. Isn't there?" My magick tingled, raising gooseflesh along my skin. I'd begun to recognize the signs of my magick working to tell me things.

"Yes." He held my gaze, a crease forming between his brows. "There's more I need to tell you. About Gadlizel."

"I get the feeling this is something a lot more."

He smiled. "It is."

"Why haven't you told me before?"

"Because I wanted you all to myself for a while. I realize now that the gods put you in my life for more than my personal happiness. Your gift...could help us."

A wash of soothing awareness flushed over me, as if Elska herself was smoothing a hand down my hair and back. I'd known this for a while.

"Yes," I agreed. "I believe you're right."

Since we'd arrived here, I'd felt the stirring of something dark deep in the mountains, the same essence I'd sensed in that nightwyrm. But there was more buried in the mountain than evil.

A power emanated deep below us. Whatever it was, that was what Vallon had not yet told me about.

He pressed a kiss to my forehead then wrapped his arms around me, holding me tight against his body. "No matter what happens, Murgha, know that I love you." He pressed his mouth to the crown of my head.

Another sweet wash of magick, the calming rush that confirmed the truths of others. Not only did I hear the words, but I knew they were true. It was the sweetest song to my heart.

"As I love you." I closed my eyes and breathed him in, savoring the moment before we were forced to face the world and whatever danger lay ahead.

Thank you for reading KINGS AND BONES. Turn the page to read the Northgall Short "A Beast Fae's Bargain" of Murgha's sister Tessa meeting her mate.

Stay tuned for news on Book 2, THE BEAST LORD, coming in 2025.

THE BEAST FAE'S BARGAIN

A RISE OF NORTHGALL SHORT

JULIETTE CROSS

A Beast Fae's Bargain

"Don't go, Tessa."

"I have to," I hissed. "Papa needs the juniper. The brew is the only thing that eases his stomach pains, and the fever is worsening."

I strode to his bedroom door. His complexion was still pale, face glistening with beads of sweat by the firelight.

"If you wait till the morning, the apothecary may have gotten more."

I scoffed, grabbing my brown satchel from the hook on the wall.

"That useless slug? Not a chance, Murgha. He's so far up the high lord's arse, he'll never care about us lowlings."

"Tessa!" My sister's pointed ears tipped red, her pink mouth downturned. "We're *not* lowlings." Her gaze fell to the floor with a flash of shame.

Then I felt a similar feeling burrowing in my chest. "No, dear," I added softly. "We are not."

Every creature in our world had its place in the hierarchy of power. Those without any magick at all were given the derogatory title, lowlings. Our mother was one of them. Papa had never let any prejudice against her slip from his lips until Murgha began to grow older, her pale white hair never darkening. Until it was obvious that Papa wasn't her real father. Until one day, he told our mother he had no use for wife who had no magick and who gave her body to other men.

Our mother had dark hair and eyes. As did Papa. As did I. But not Murgha. Her pale features, white hair, and violet eyes were the trademark of high-born moon fae from Lumeria. Though she had no wings like the moon fae, the rest of her features were a beacon that she had one of their kind's blood running through her veins.

I'd hated Papa that day, sitting on the front stoop of our drab little inn with a five-year-old Murgha wailing in my lap while we both watched him threaten to kill our mother if she came back. She walked away, staring back at us with tears in her eyes. She never denied that Murgha was the child of another man. And that man never showed up to claim her as his own.

Not long after, Papa moved us into another clan of wood fae on the eastern border of Lumeria. Later, I realized he wanted to go where she couldn't find us. He got his wish. She never did.

It wasn't kind of me to use the lowling slur at all, even in jest. But it was obvious that our clan—a small cluster of wood fae living as far away from Issos as possible—was at the bottom of the feeding trough.

Wood fae weren't nomadic clans by nature but we'd followed our high lord's advice to leave the Midland when the war between the Wraith King and the Lumerians closer to Myrkovir Forest where we lived. We'd settled here in this territory on the outskirts of the Borderlands, preferring to be far from the ongoing war where the wraith king's black-clad warriors roamed the land, burning villages as they went.

Unfortunately, we also lived far too close to Gadlizel and Meerland—the darklands ruled by demon fae and all manner of monsters.

Feeling guilty for upsetting Murgha, I walked over and pulled her into my arms on a heavy sigh.

"No, Mur. We're not lowlings. But our clan is all but forgotten. Too far from Lumeria to matter, and the shadows continue to gather."

She clutched at my back, her fingers curling into my home-spun blouse. "Which is exactly why you should *not* go." Her voice dropped to a breathless whisper. "I'm getting those itchy feelings again."

Her magick was latent, just starting to manifest at seventeen, and so far, we didn't know what kind of magick it was. Her skin itched when she thought bad things were going to happen. Like right before father fell ill, she'd itched her inner arm so badly, I'd had to wrap it with a poultice.

But no wood fae had ever manifested the gift of an oracle, and oracles didn't predict omens with rashes and such. I was afraid that perhaps Murgha had no magick at all, that this was all a figment of her imagination. But I wouldn't let my sweet little sister think herself a lowling, a curse for our kind.

"Besides," she whispered ominously, "The beast fae have been seen."

I shivered. The beast fae were one of the most feared of magick kind. They were neither fae nor animal, but something in between. Long ago, a warped shadow fae witch seduced a lone Meer-wolf. From their mating, she gave birth to a brood of half-animal creatures. They multiplied into a monstrous species. They are hideous to behold and fiercely deadly, constantly craving blood and their next meal of flesh.

Of course, I'd never seen one. If I had, I'd be dead.

Putting on a fake smile, I eased back and gripped her slender shoulders.

"Well," I said lightly, "at least it's not King Gollaya himself."

Murgha gasped, her face going white at the mere mention of the Wraith King.

She spat over her left then right shoulder, then touched her thumb to forehead, chin, and chest, all in two seconds. A charm to keep demon magick out of her mind, mouth, and heart.

"Don't even joke about such things, Tessa."

I grabbed the fileting knife I used to gut and clean our fish, waved it at Murgha and stuffed it in my belt.

"There's a juniper bush near the fork of the stream. I'll have what I need and be back in an hour. Lock the door behind me."

Before she could say another word, I was gone. I paused only long enough to hear the bolt slide home.

"Good, little sister," I muttered before I launched into a sprint toward the woodlands behind our cabin.

Though our house was comfortable, I missed our home in the Midlands. We lived in tree houses in the tops of an oak grove. That's where we belonged. Everything was backward now. Ever since we left, we'd lost something more than our home. It was like we'd lost ourselves the farther we migrated away from the center of the light fae world—Lumeria.

Shrugging off our old woes, I focused on my current one. It was warm now that we'd settled into early summer. A balmy night breeze blew through my hair as I ran. I'd worn a short-sleeved blouse tucked into my thinnest skirt, foregoing undergarments altogether.

I had no breasts to speak of, not like Murgha, even though I was five years older than her. There was no point in wearing a corset, and unless it was my bleeding time, I preferred to be free beneath my skirt.

Attuning my magick to what I needed, it guided me through the dark, my path lit only by the half-moon above. My skirt billowed freely around my ankles as I drew closer, the gurgling of the brook filtering through the night sounds of a hooting owl and buzzing insects.

Coming into the open of a small clearing, I slowed my steps toward the thick old oak stretching tall and wide next to a boulder.

"Good evening, Mr. Oak and Ms. Stone. Still carrying on your little affair, I see."

Smiling, I sauntered toward the boulder through the short grass that grew close to the brook.

"Well, don't mind me. I won't interrupt you for long. You'll pardon me, Ms. Stone," I said, kneeling at the slanted side of her where the tiny, evergreen bush of juniper berries sprouted. "I simply need a few of these, and I'll be on my way."

Removing the fileting knife at my belt and the satchel from my shoulder, I set to work, cutting sprigs carefully and storing them quickly.

That's when I realized there was no sound above the murmuring creek. No owl hooting. Not even insects buzzing. The hairs on the back of my neck stood on end, my magick prickling along my skin, recognizing the aura of its kind in the air.

I stood and spun, thrusting my sharp blade in front of me.

A pair of glowing yellow eyes high in the tree line stared back at me. At first, I thought it some kind of night creature hovering in the low branches but then the owner of that set of glowing eyes stepped forward into the patch of moonlight and my breath hitched.

Standing seven feet tall, taller counting the tips of his four horns, was a dark fae—a muscular one vibrating with potent magick. He was shirtless and wore nothing but a leather skirt around his waist that hung to near his knees, revealing an expanse of bronzed amber skin.

His thighs were bare, but a thicker pelt of fine fur started at his knees, covering his lower legs to his claw-tipped feet.

Rune tattoos swirled over his forehead and across his broad chest which was also sprinkled with fine fur down the backs of his forearms. His four horns, two thicker than the others, curled backward and swooped up at the tips, both beautiful and menacing. He wore jewelry, piercings trailing up his ears, silver encircling the base of his horns and also his wrists. He was important.

Was he royal?

He stepped closer, slowly, carefully, while I still held my knife in front of me. It was comical to think I could defend myself against such a huge, powerful beast, but I'd die trying if I must.

While his gaze raked me with intense scrutiny—a low purr rumbling in his chest—he made no sudden moves to attack. Then he spoke and my knees wobbled.

"What are you doing here, fair one?"

His voice, deep and sonorous and unfairly seductive, rumbled along my skin, raising gooseflesh as it swept over me. But it was a shiver of fear that trembled down my spine when I caught a glimpse of sharp teeth.

"You're a beast fae," was all I managed to spit out, voice shaking.

A long tail covered in fine pelt fur and a thicker tuft at the tip flicked behind him close to the ground. He inclined his head as if I complimented him, his giant, claw-tipped feet taking a circling step toward me. Corralling his prey, it seemed.

"And you are a lovely wood fae female…all alone in the middle of the woods at night."

Then he smiled, revealing his four sharp canine teeth, and I truly understood the meaning of fear.

"Please don't eat me," I blurted, my hand shaking where I held out the knife.

His smile widened. "I can't make any promises."

Squeezing my eyes shut, I shot a prayer to Elska, Goddess of the Wood. Then snapped them open, keeping my eyes fixed on the slowly circling beast fae.

I couldn't believe I was actually looking at one. He wasn't hideous. I expected a malformed face and snarling yellow teeth dripping slobber and blood and the flesh of his last meal. Though his nose and mouth jutted out more than a normal fae's face and his forehead was more prominent, it was interesting and oddly…attractive.

"You shouldn't be in these woods at night, fair one."

"I needed the juniper for my father. He's sick."

"A good and obedient daughter."

"Most of the time," I admitted, thinking if I kept talking, he wouldn't want to maul me and drink my blood.

"Does my appearance offend you?"

"No," I answered honestly. "But you don't look like I thought you would."

"What had you expected?" he stopped moving, now in front of the great oak's trunk, his tail flicking slowly behind him as he studied me.

"Something…uglier."

His canines flashed again with another smile, and I wondered at my reckless behavior, telling him everything I thought and felt. A strange tug at the center of my chest compelled me to open to him.

"What is your name?" he asked in that same deep, silky voice.

"Tessa." Again, the impulse to give him what he wanted, to please him, both confused and disturbed me. "Do you have the magick of compulsion?"

His brow lifted in surprise. "My kind do not have that sort of magick."

"Is it true?" I asked, my hand lowering slightly. "That your ancestor was a shadow fae witch who mated with a Meer-wolf."

Amusement crinkled his eyes as his chest rumbled with low laughter. "My, my." He shook his head, easing a single step closer. "Have you ever seen a Meer-wolf?"

"No." Of course I hadn't. Their packs lived in the northeast, far from where I'd lived most my life.

"They are as tall as a Pallasian stallion, some even taller, and twice as thick." Pallasian horses stood twelve to fifteen feet tall. "A Meer-wolf's fangs are as long as you are from here to here." He pointed from his inner elbow to the end of his wrist. "And though some of the wolves are tamed by our hand, they would not mate with a fae. Nor would a fae desire to mate with an animal."

His look turned to something like pity mixed with disgust.

"I'm sorry if I offended you." Because the last thing I needed to do was make this demon fae angry. "That's what our elders say."

"The all-knowing light fae elders." He quirked his brow haughtily. "They mislead you."

"How did you get to be..." I gestured toward his body. My hand shook where it still held out the knife, my sad attempt at defense against a beast fae. A high-ranking one. "Like you are."

"Cursed." His golden eyes flared brighter with a pulse of magick.

I bit my lip to keep from whimpering at the dazzling sensation of his magick caressing my skin. It was like no magick I'd ever sensed before, a pleasurable hum of potent energy dancing across my exposed arms, neck and face, trying to burrow beneath my skin to the flesh beneath.

"Cursed by whom?" I asked, voice shaky again.

"A light fae priestess. Long ago." He tilted his head, drawing my attention to his magnificent set of horns. "The beast fae are children of the demon god Vix and his fae consort Mizrah. We have always had an affinity for animals, particularly Meer-wolves, our magick more akin to their senses."

"How do you mean?"

"We are excellent hunters. Our magick enhances these senses," was his quick reply, his yellow eyes glinting brightly. "But then a moon fae priestess cursed our people to look more like the wolves we so loved, like the beasts we revered. So we would be reviled by fae-kind."

I blinked at this astonishing revelation. I believed he was telling the truth. "That's not at all what my kinsmen have said of your kind."

"Of course not. Then the blame for our monstrous appearance," he gestured down his body, "would be set upon them. Rather than ourselves."

My gaze wandered down his torso yet again, my pulse pounding faster at the sight of his thick, muscular thighs and arms, his broad chest as wide as the medicine cabinet in our kitchen. He was made of slabs of muscle, his hair thick, almost fur-like along his calves and thickest near his giant clawed feet. I realized I was rudely staring, but I couldn't help it. I'd never seen any fae so powerfully built in all my life.

"Perhaps the lady would rather see all of this beast fae, to feed her curiosity," he said in that deep, sonorous voice.

"No, that's not necessary. I—"

Within a blink, he unwrapped the leather skirt at his waist

and tossed it aside, now completely, shamelessly naked before me.

"*Mother of stars*," I muttered, my breath sucked from my chest.

A thick thatch of hair covered his chest as well but not completely, thinning to a narrow line beneath his naval. The rippling muscle and broad pectorals could easily be seen, but it was what hung semi-erect between his thick thighs that had my jaw dropping.

"You, y—" I licked my lips trying to summon saliva into my mouth so my tongue would stop sticking to the roof of it, "you can put that back on."

I pointed aimlessly off to the side with the tip of my blade, my eyes still devouring every hard inch of him.

"I prefer it this way. I like that look on your face."

Trying to school my features into some semblance of calm, I forced my gaze to his face and tried to keep it there.

"Besides," he shrugged in that slow, easy mannerism, "I have no shame of my body."

Heavens above, he had no reason to be ashamed.

He circled the outer perimeter of the clearing, seemingly moving farther away, but I knew what he was doing. He was attempting to calm his prey, to ease me into letting my guard down. What could I do anyway? If I ran, he'd catch me and over-power me. If I fought, he'd subdue me. It was understood between the both of us. So I had to use my brains instead.

"I am not a maiden," I blurted.

His mouth quirked, biceps flexing. "Why do you tell me this?"

"Because we know that beast fae seek virgins to satisfy their appetites."

"You know this?" he asked, arching a sable brow.

He was mocking me. "It is known. The elders tell of it."

"Ah." He gave a definitive nod, dragging my attention to the four horns curling almost regally around his head like a crown. "Well, if the elders tell of it, it must be true."

"You're making fun of me. Are you saying this is not true?"

His yellow eyes flashed. "I need no virgin to satisfy my appetites." He continued to pace closer.

"You will not force me then?"

"I could," he said so cavalierly. "Your scent is intoxicating."

Stars above. He could smell me, and I was well aware that the sight of his naked form had stirred arousal. The mention of my scent warmed me further between my thighs.

He purred with a low, "Mmmm."

He stopped several feet from me, locking his stance wide, his arms casually at his side. But I knew he could burst into action and tackle me before I could even open my mouth to scream. Who would hear me out here anyway?

"But will you?" I asked, voice high and nervous, pulse pounding faster. "Force me?"

Tension built of both fear and arousal stretched between us. And I couldn't fathom how I was feeling both of these sensations, my body tightening as if anticipating some great event.

He tilted his head again in that almost animalistic way, a predator sizing up prey.

"It is not our way," he said casually then, "Let us play a game."

"What kind of a game?" I asked in a whisper.

"One where if I win you give me your body willingly."

"My body?" Though I knew what he meant, I couldn't help but ask for clarification.

"You lay with me," he clarified.

He said it so casually that I should've been revolted, but somehow it didn't have the effect I thought it would. I kept my gaze on his, too afraid to let it drift too far south. I was already struggling to think straight.

"You say that so casually. Like its nothing at all to have inter-course with someone."

"It's rather the opposite," he stated, those golden eyes glimmering brighter. "To share your body with another is as close to the divine we can achieve on this earth. I'd say that isn't nothing."

How could this beast fae speak so philosophically, so poetically, about sex? I found myself wondering what that would feel like to lay with a creature like him.

I'd had two lovers before. The apothecary's son Finleal was my first. He was sweet and tender, but obviously as inexperienced as I was. Then there was a fae warrior Melkin last year. He and his regiment were passing through from Issos on their way to Morodon. They'd rested from their long journey with our clan for two weeks before moving on. Melkin was more masculine and satisfying in bed than Finleal.

And yet, I couldn't help wondering if this beast fae had more to offer. Murgha always said I was too reckless, too excited for adventure for my own good. She was right.

I scoffed and lifted my chin defiantly. "You plan to cheat."

He held his right hand over his naked chest over his heart. "I swear on Lumera. I will not."

"I don't pray to the moon goddess." I arched my own brow in a haughty retort. "And neither do you, beast fae."

His lips quirked, then his expression lightened with curiosity. "Who do you pray to?"

"Elska. Goddess of the Wood, of course." His gaze remained transfixed on me. "You don't know much about the light fae, do you?"

"I've never met one before. Until you." His gaze dipped along the line of my body before returning to my own. "Now back to our game."

"How do we play?"

"You do nothing, but let me kiss you."

"That's not a game. How does one of us win?"

"Easy. If you make no noise at all, then you win. But if you make any sound of pleasure, I win and can take my prize."

"What if I make a sound of disgust?"

He grinned. Long, sharp canines on top and bottom gleamed white under the moonlight. "Then you win. I'll even escort you home, unmolested."

"So if I win, if I make no sound of...of pleasure, then you escort me home."

He dipped his horns. "And if I win, you give yourself to me."

This was madness. I could hear Murgha shrieking a protest if she were here, telling me how reckless and foolish I always was.

But Murgha wasn't here. And this enticing beast fae was. And what other choice did I have? Perhaps if I lay with him, he'd let me live. And that dark spark that lived in the heart of me was taunting my spirit with temptation. The kind I never walked away from.

"What is your name?" I asked.

"Will you consent to the game?" he asked, dodging my question.

"Are you a lord of your kind?" My gaze flicked to the silver cuffs on his wrists and the ones around his horns. "Are you a king?"

He eased forward, now only a foot from me. "No. I am chief warrior to one."

A warrior. There would be no fighting my way out. My breath hitched as I gazed far up at him. He was easily two feet taller than me, his horns making him three.

"Lean back onto the rock, sweet Tessa."

Without ever agreeing to his game, I found myself gripping

the slanted stone behind me and laying back. My mind might be screaming to run, but my body wanted to play.

He knelt before me, still towering higher than me even on his knees. His hands gripped the bottom hem of my skirt and lifted.

"What are you doing?"

I grabbed his forearm right above the circlet of silver, magick reverberating through my body with a tremor of power. His magick wanted inside me. I could feel it. I wanted it inside me.

"You said just a kiss," I protested though it was a weak protest.

"And that's all it will be if you win. But I did not say where the kiss would be placed. And you did not ask."

"Demon's trick," I hissed.

"Always, fair one."

His honey-gold eyes locked on mine as he began lifting the hem of my skirt, the pads of his fingers trailing along the sides of my calves, my knees, then my thighs.

"Lean back, my sweet," he crooned through those devilish fanged teeth, his molten gaze hot on mine.

I did as he commanded and leaned back on the stone, letting my head fall to the hard rock, my arms and hands splayed at my sides. His mouth quirked up as he lifted my skirt to my waist, his gaze finally dropping to the apex of my thighs.

A deep, guttural growl rumbled in his chest. "So lovely." He coasted his thumbs along the seam of my thighs and pussy.

He leaned forward, his mouth open as he took a deep inhale, his golden eyes closing with pleasure. Then he opened them and pierced me to the stone at my back.

"Not a sound, my sweet. Or I win."

Then he leaned forward and flicked out his tongue. My breath hitched. His tongue was so very long, abnormally so. He kept my gaze and spread the folds of my pussy then circled the tight nub between, his eyes sliding shut on a groan.

I sucked in a breath and bit my lip, my body thrumming with maddening pleasure. I tightened my fists on the stone, biting my lip so hard I tasted a metallic drop of blood.

"Not a sound," he whispered against my pussy then opened his mouth over it and sucked slowly, deeply, salaciously.

"Stars save me," I muttered.

His grin slid wide while he continued to lick in a slow, circular rhythm. "Awfully close to a sound of pleasure," he breathed hotly.

I squeezed my eyes shut and tilted my head back, arching my neck as he continued with his erotic kiss. His magick sizzled along my skin, vibrating through flesh and bones, melting me from the inside out. It was as if this wild fae was meant to kneel at my feet and worship me this way.

How can that be?

I tried so hard, inhaling deep to keep any sound from escaping my mouth.

But by the heavens, there was no ignoring the mind-blurring, body-trembling pleasure trembling through me. His velvet tongue was coaxing my spirit into his keeping. I wanted to crawl into his lap then inside him. What a bizarre feeling.

He lapped softly then slid his long tongue inside me, thrusting while lifting one of my thighs wider, his clawed hand wrapped entirely around my thigh near my knee.

By the gods, there was no winning this game. And strangely, I didn't want to. I wanted this beast fae, his magick skimming along my body, his power over me, inside me, begging to wholly possess me.

I rocked my pelvis up, thrusting my pussy against his mouth and whimpered a moan. His answering groan was one of triumph as he lapped at my swollen bud.

When I lifted my head and opened my eyes lazily, he lifted his own. "I believe I've won," he whispered in a low, deep purr, his mouth sliding into the wickedest smile.

"Yes," I agreed, knowing I was consenting to more than him winning our little game.

In a flash, he'd scooped me off of the rock and lay me on the tufted grass near the gurgling brook. He was so massive, he completely engulfed me, caging me against the forest floor with his huge body. He spread my thigh open with his knee as slid the broad length of his cock along the folds of my pussy.

"Open for me," he demanded gruffly. "I must get inside you." It was the first time he'd appeared untamed or close to the savage I'd imagined.

I let my other thigh fall wide then reached up and instinctively gripped his two largest horns.

"That's it, fair one." He swept his wide mouth against mine. "Hold onto your demon while he rides you hard."

I hitched in a breath when the head of his cock pressed inside me. He was so much larger than my former lovers. When he thrust in a few more inches, I whimpered at the uncomfortable size of him.

"Shhh," he whispered near my ear before licking and nipping my neck with teeth, slowing his entrance. "You can take me, fair one. Relax and let me inside."

His crooning words and lapping kisses sent a spike of arousal through me. I rocked up, taking him deeper.

"Yes, my sweet. Just like that." Then he pumped deeper, stretching me until he was fully seated. "Perfect."

"It's so tight," I breathed on a gasp.

He rumbled a growl. "Absolutely perfect."

Then he withdrew to the tip slowly and stroked back in on a hiss, slow and easy. My arousal increased with every heavy thrust, my body sizzling with such intense pleasure I thought perhaps this was his true magick, this brain-hazing, rapturous sex.

He lapped at my shoulder as he fucked me harder, deeper, my moans echoing up to the trees. His tail coiled around my thigh, close to the knee, holding me wide.

I moaned and pressed my breasts against his chest with each of his dipping thrusts, my nipples peaked and aching beneath the fabric.

Suddenly, he hauled me up as he rocked back onto his heels. Curling his body over me, he ripped my blouse open and sucked my nipple, grazing with sharp teeth.

"Ah!" I gripped my thighs around his torso as he pumped up inside me, his mouth on my breast. Then my head fell back as a reeling orgasm shattered through me, my pussy quivering around his thick cock. "Yes!"

His growl would've terrified me if I didn't know it stemmed from extreme pleasure. His clawed hand cradled my head, his arm wrapped tightly around my waist as he fucked me with deep, slow thrusts. His mouth hovered against my lips, his feral gaze locked on mine, a startling ferocity sparking there.

"Oh, fair one." His voice trembled as did his jagged exhale as something began to happen.

His cock seemed to swell even more at the base, and I realized with an odd sensation of both dread and longing what it was. I'd heard that beast fae knotted their women, tethering them together during sex. But the knot only formed for one woman. His mate.

"Is that...what I think it is?" I whispered against his wide, grinning mouth.

"Yes, my sweet." He ground his cock inside me, the knot

swelling bigger to near painful pressure. His golden eyes flashed with new intensity. "You're mine, sweet Tessa."

Then he roared up to the trees, his giant cock spilling inside me. I whimpered in his arms, still gripping his horns as if it gave me some power over him, as if I could master this formidable, magnificent creature.

His head dropped back to my throat and shoulder where he lapped, a deep groan pouring through him, vibrating against my chest. Then I felt the prick of pain in my shoulder as he sank his fangs into the muscle.

"Ah!" I jerked in his arms but he held me tighter, his moan humming against my skin as he sucked my blood. "Oh, gods. What is happening?"

He made no reply but the silky, satisfied hum of ecstasy as he held me tight, his cock knotted deep, and lapped at the bite mark on my shoulder. A tingling sensation—his magick—eased the pain.

My mind drifted in a haze of pleasure and pain together, the experience more sublime than anything I'd ever known.

Sometime later, though I couldn't tell how long, he rocked us forward, my back landing on the plush grass again, my clothes half torn off me. He pulled his cock from my body with a jarring pop, a rush of his semen spilling out.

He cradled the back of my skull while he reached down between us and spread our mess over my overly sensitive clitoris. I whimpered and tried to get away.

"I've got you, sweet Tessa." He continued to pet me down below. "I had not thought this night would bring such a treasure to me." Then he surged forward, imprisoning me with his large body, and pressed his wide mouth to mine, kissing me with soft laps of his tongue.

I mewled and squirmed, arousal humming yet again. "By the

gods, what is happening to me?"

He pressed his forehead to mine for a brief moment. "It has already happened, my treasure." He righted my torn dress as best he could then scooped me into his arms and stood.

"Hallizel," he called up to the trees, his eyes still on mine. "Ghasta met."

Demon tongue.

A wood sprite flew down from the boughs of the oak, fluttering its transparent wings, birdlike talons hooked beneath its small, femininely shaped body. I'd seen them before though not this close. Its eyes were round and full black, its body midnight blue, almost black, with a pearlescent sheen even to the tips of its pointed ears. Tiny feathers wisped up at the base of its smooth, downy head.

He spoke a string of words in demon tongue to the faerie creature then it flitted off into the night.

"What did you tell her?" I asked, looping my arms around his thick neck, my body and spirit floating in a euphoric state.

"She will get the medicine to your father for you."

"How will she know where to go?"

"She will follow your scent back to your home."

I stared at him, soaking in his otherworldly beauty. Yes. Now that fear didn't cloud my vision, I could see how truly beautiful he was.

"What is your name?"

His mouth quirked. "I am Bezaliel."

"And where am I going?" I asked, somehow calm and serene, not terrified as I should be.

"Wherever I go, sweet Tessa." He nuzzled his broad nose against mine, inhaling deeply. "Wherever I go."

"But my sister? And how can I live with you? Your kind hate mine."

"Another truth from your elders?"

When I said nothing, his mouth quirked as he carried me into the thick woods.

"My kind hate no one, though they are cautious of everyone. They will accept you because you are mine. Which means you are their kind as well."

"What about my sister?"

"I will watch over her. From afar."

"But not too far."

"Not too far," he assured me.

I pressed my body closer and snuggled my head beneath his chin as he walked deeper into the dark woods, the moon disappearing behind the canopy of trees.

I couldn't say what exactly had happened, how I had changed so drastically from the woman who feared the dark fae to the woman who willingly accepted her fate as this dark warrior's mate, willingly abandoning her family for him. But I knew down to the deep marrow of my bones that this was right. That he was mine as much as I was his. I had no other choice. My place was with him.

While he said his people would accept me, I knew that mine would kill him on sight if we tried to return to my village.

My magick hummed with joy as I sighed against his neck.

"Wherever you go, Bezaliel."

He purred with satisfaction as he cradled me tighter against him, kissing the crown of my head as he walked on into the dark.

Follow JULIETTE *on social media and subscribe to her newsletter for upcoming release news, including book 2 in THE RISE OF NORTHGALL series—THE BEAST LORD, coming in 2025.*

www.ingramcontent.com/pod-product-compliance
Lightning Source LLC
Chambersburg PA
CBHW060455300726
48975CB00008B/2524